"Here's where everyone's been hiding."

Rory appeared in the doorway, wearing an outfit similar to her daughter's, red T-shirt under overalls, but minus the boots and crown. "Funny how when it's time to clean up, everyone disappears. Even the dog."

Sarge yipped as if putting up a defense at her accusation and her face split into a soft smile.

Mitch swallowed hard and his heart rate kicked up at the sight of that smile. It may have been directed at Sarge, but he was the one reacting to it. He had to remind himself that he hadn't come here looking to get involved with a woman. Especially one with a child. He needed to remember his plan to live a selfish life. Anyone responsible for a child didn't have the luxury of selfish behavior. So that right there disqualified him.

He blamed his reaction to Rory on the situation. His earlier reactions had softened him up. Yep, that was it. He had come to Loon Lake to look for his dog. Nothing more. He wasn't looking for a relationship. Or a family.

His dog was all he wanted...wasn't it?

Dear Reader,

As a writer, I have learned that stories sometimes take on a life of their own. Although this was always Mitch and Rory's story, certain aspects changed from the time I first imagined the book and I started writing it. As it turned out, Sarge the dog had an even bigger part than I first imagined, but it required he lose a leg. Oh, Carrie, how could you? While I honestly regretted Sarge's missing limb, the veterinarian I spoke with assured me dogs can live happy, full lives on three legs. Unlike people, dogs don't regret what might have been but simply live life to the fullest. Maybe that's what my characters needed to learn. So, while Sarge may have lost something, he's contributing not only to the story but to the lives of the people he adores and who love him in return.

Not only do stories take on a life of their own, but characters as well. I know it probably sounds strange, but characters sometimes do things that surprise me. At one point in the story, Mitch started doing something and I kept thinking, "No, Mitch, don't do that!" but he insisted. What he did was right for the character and the story, but it was totally his decision. Let's see if you can guess which scene that was. I'd love to hear from you at authorcarrienichols@gmail.com.

Carrie Nichols

A Hero and His Dog

CARRIE NICHOLS

HARLEQUIN
SPECIAL
EDITION

HARLEQUIN®
SPECIAL EDITION™

ISBN-13: 978-1-335-72442-7

A Hero and His Dog

Harlequin Enterprises ULC
22 Adelaide St. West, 41st Floor
Toronto, Ontario M5H 4E3, Canada
www.Harlequin.com

Printed in U.S.A.

Recycling programs for this product may not exist in your area.

Carrie Nichols grew up in New England but moved south and traded snow for central AC. She loves to travel, is addicted to British crime dramas and knows a *Seinfeld* quote appropriate for every occasion.

A 2016 RWA Golden Heart® Award winner and two-time Maggie Award for Excellence winner, she has one tolerant husband, two grown sons and two critical cats. To her dismay, Carrie's characters—like her family—often ignore the wisdom and guidance she offers.

Books by Carrie Nichols

Harlequin Special Edition

Small-Town Sweethearts

Visit the Author Profile page
at Harlequin.com for more titles.

This one is for my editor, Carly Silver,
because this book is just as much hers as mine.
Carly, thank you for being my editor and
bringing out the best in not only my stories
but me as a writer. You will be missed.

Chapter One

Mitch Sawicki's foot itched. Not a problem—*if* he could scratch it. But he'd left that foot, along with the lower half of the same leg, behind in the Afghan desert. The surgeon had referred to his surgery as a *transtibial amputation*, which meant the leg below the knee was removed. They'd assured him that there'd be less atrophy of his muscles and retaining his knee would provide greater balance and stability. He sighed because none of that reassuring news provided relief from the current itchiness as he stood on this farmhouse porch.

Above or below the knee didn't alter the bottom line. His career working with his canine partner as a combat engineer with the 75th Ranger Regiment was over, changing forever the person he used to be. He was still in the process of figuring out who this new Mitch was.

He reached for the rubber band he liked to wear around his wrist for when these phantom sensations occurred before remembering he'd left it in the cupholder back in his truck. It wasn't worth going back to get it. Snapping the band was painful, but it served to redirect his brain. He preferred the fleeting sting of the band to the nausea and drowsiness caused by the Gabapentin the doctors had prescribed to alter the neurotransmitters in his brain. Hoping to redirect the impulses and relieve the annoying itch without medical intervention, he pinched and massaged his thigh.

These phantom sensations, caused by the nerves left intact, were part of his new reality, just one of the things he'd been learning to live with this past year. Which meant he coped and kept quiet because people tended to give him disbelieving looks if he talked about it. Why was it so hard for others to believe he could feel sensations in the missing limb other than pain?

His prosthetic wasn't visible beneath the drab olive fatigue pants he wore today, so the person answering the door wouldn't be any the wiser. Unless they had X-ray vision. He snort-laughed at that absurd thought and pressed the doorbell.

Concentrate on the mission, Sawicki.

He tensed at the sound of running footsteps from inside the home. *Running?* The blue-painted wooden door swung open to reveal… Nothing?

Movement had Mitch redirecting his gaze downward. A tiny, waif-like girl, no more than three or four years old, stood smiling up at him. Dressed in a flowing gown of some sort of glittery pink material and a crown of crushed aluminum foil, she looked as though she'd stepped off the pages of one of those Little Golden Books. On her feet were shiny red rubber boots. Make that a fractured fairy tale.

"Hi, I'm Phoebe," the girl chirped, her dark eyes large in her round, cherubic face.

Flummoxed, he stared mutely at her. He'd been psyching himself for this encounter for the past eight hundred miles, determined to get results, make demands if necessary. All done as politely as possible of course, but nonetheless he'd stand firm even if one of the feet he'd be standing on was a product of modern medical science. Failure was not an option. If the dog he saw on that video was indeed his former partner, he was getting Sarge back.

In the scenario in his head, the door would be opened by an adult, someone he could reason with. Preferably that former marine from the video so he could appeal to his sense of honor regarding a previous partner. Except Mitch hadn't prepared himself for this. Nothing could have.

He might have first-hand combat experience but talking to this young girl was more nerve wracking than coming under fire in an urban setting. Facing someone with a rifle he could handle, but a child?

"Mister? You're supposed to tell me your name

now. Mommy says it's called *being polite*," Phoebe said in a gentle but scolding tone.

"Mitch," he replied, his lips twitching as he contemplated the miniature Ms. Manners.

"Phoebe!" A husky but unmistakably feminine voice scolded the child from somewhere in the house but was coming closer. "What have I told you about waiting for me before you open the door?"

Mitch dragged his gaze upward to a harried-looking woman scurrying down a long hallway toward them. She draped the towel she'd been using to wipe her hands over her shoulder and stepped behind the girl. No shiny boots or tinfoil crowns, she was dressed conservatively in faded jeans and a white button-down shirt tucked into the pants. Even so, with her coffee-brown eyes, dark curly hair, and rosy cheeks she was an adult version of the child. His attention—and his imagination—was captured by a twinkle in her liquid brown eyes. That gleam made it seem as if she were harboring some intriguing secrets. Secrets he wanted to investigate. Once again, he was having trouble gathering his thoughts and forming words.

"Uh-oh, Mr. Mitch. We broke a rule." The child peered up at him, her smile guileless even as she dragged him into her transgression.

Mitch's resolve began to weaken. Huh. Evidently it wasn't as absolute as he'd once thought.

"*You* broke the rule, Miss Phoebe," the woman corrected and put a possessive hand on Phoebe's bony shoulder. "We have that rule because you don't know who could be on the other side of the door."

The girl twisted to glance up at the woman. "But, Mommy, that's why you hafta opens it. To see who's there. And I did." Turning back, the fairy princess scowled and pointed an accusing finger. "That's Mitch. *He* was there when I opened it."

He sucked in a breath, preparing to apologize for being on the other side of the door, but shut his mouth with a click of his teeth. What the heck was he doing? Making apologies was *not* part of the plan. He'd been prepared to go mano a mano with the person who'd taken possession of his K9 partner. Whether that person was the crusty former marine from the news video that had sent him on his journey, or some mysterious navy lieutenant who was claiming to be Sarge's owner.

The truth was, he hadn't prepared for a girl in red rubber boots and tinfoil crown instructing him on the finer points of polite conversation. He began to doubt his ability to complete this mission. Prior to his injuries he'd never doubted accomplishing anything he'd set out to do. He'd had his share of self-confidence, some might have gone so far as to call it arrogance, but it had served him well. It had gotten him through the final, most grueling part of Ranger school—the so-called swamp phase. So why was he letting these two throw him off his game?

He was capable of changing a failing strategy while facing intense enemy fire and yet these two had him groping for words. He needed to—

"Are you here about the job?" the woman asked.

"The job?" he parroted.

Because of the flat vowels in her speech, he assumed she was a New England native, because who the hell else would have intentionally moved to Loon Lake, a mere dot in the map of central Vermont. Just one more place where he was an outsider. Just as he'd been during his twelve years in that desert. Other than short visits to see his mom, he hadn't spent much time in his native Chicago since graduating high school and enlisting in the army.

Suspicion and curiosity flitted across her face, furrowing her brow and creating a sexy little indentation above her nose.

What would it feel like if he used his finger—or better yet, his tongue—to explore that little groove? *Damn.* That thought was as disconcerting as it was reassuring. Between the extended hospitalizations for his injuries and his broken engagement, sex had taken a back seat in both his life and his thoughts. But this wasn't the time or place for the resurgence of his once-dormant libido.

He adjusted the weight on his prosthetic. *Concentrate on the mission, Sawicki.*

For nearly a year he'd believed the initial information he'd been given that his canine partner hadn't survived the attack on their convoy. Until two days ago; that's when he'd first watched a YouTube video from a rural Vermont news station. It was a human-interest story about a three-legged dog foiling a purse snatching. Despite lacking a limb, the dog had chased down the would-be thief and wrestled the purse back.

The television crew had interviewed the middle-aged former marine who'd brought the dog to the park. But Mitch's attention had been focused on the animal, a Belgian Tervuren, which resembled a shaggy version of a German shepherd. The caption across the bottom of the screen had identified the man as former gunnery sergeant Walt Griffin. The man had said the dog belonged to his nephew, Navy Lieutenant Bowie Griffin, adding that Sarge was a former MWD: Military Working Dog. Not only the breed but the fact he'd been a MWD had caught Mitch's eye and had been the reason an army buddy had initially sent him the video link.

That last bit of information and watching the video over and over had clinched it for Mitch. He'd thrown clothes and toiletries into his battered duffel bag and made the thirteen-hour drive from Fayetteville, North Carolina, near Fort Bragg to Loon Lake in central Vermont.

Sarge had been more to Mitch than the dog he'd been assigned to handle. They'd worked side-by-side for six years and the love and trust between man and dog had been mutual. If alive, did Sarge think that Mitch had abandoned him?

"… You're not what I was expecting," the woman was saying.

Her voice jerked him back to the present and his mission.

"Honestly, you're not what I expected either." The words had left his mouth before his brain could censor them. Great. What was he, twelve, and engaging in a game of I-know-you-are-but-what-am-I?

He opened his mouth, but before he could apologize for his unfortunate retort, she was speaking again.

"I apologize, that was rude. But I posted the ad on the bulletin board at the high school library. So, frankly, I was expecting a teenager looking to earn some extra cash over the summer not…not um… you." Color rose in her face and she slapped a hand over her mouth as if trying to prevent more from rushing forth.

Did he look as though he needed to compete with high schoolers for jobs? Sure, he'd lost muscle mass, but lying in a hospital for months on end tended to do that do a guy. He'd always been sinewy instead of brawny. But now he was plain old lanky, his belt a necessary accessory.

The most accurate description of what he was today was *former*. A former Ranger thanks to last month's honorable discharge. His decision to leave the military, not theirs. A former fiancée, thanks to Cynthie's inability to handle his injuries and his new reality. Her decision that time, but, despite it being ego deflating, he'd been secretly relieved and hadn't done anything to get her to change her mind.

The biggest and most regrettable *former* he laid claim to was as Sarge's partner. He'd been told his K9 partner hadn't survived the blast that had cost him his leg. Mitch had believed what he'd been told and hadn't bothered to verify the information or track down the dog's whereabouts…until now. Shame on him. Not that there would have been a lot he could have done from his hospital bed. Except recover quicker, worked harder at PT to make it back to Sarge. The army might have been the owner of record, but Mitch had always felt Sarge was his and he would've fought tooth and nail to see that Sarge came to him once they were both released from military duty.

That was then and this was now. A little late, but he was doing something about it now. If this was *his* Sarge, the dog needed him as much as he needed the dog. How could these people know what it was like to lose a limb?

Her last comment finally penetrated through his jumble of thoughts. "You posted a help wanted ad on a bulletin board?"

What the hell, Sawicki? Never mind the job. That's not why you're here. The primary object of this mission was getting information about the dog. To find out if *this* Belgian Tervuren was his old partner. If Sarge had survived, Mitch wouldn't rest until the dog was back where he belonged. And that was with him. He had nothing against this unknown Lieutenant Griffin, but that guy hadn't worked side by side, in some of the most grueling conditions, with Sarge for over six years.

"Didn't I just say that's what I did?" she asked.

Her scowl brought back that tempting furrow in her brow. Never before had a woman's annoyance with him garnered a sexual reaction. *Get a grip*, he cautioned himself.

"Uh-oh. Mommy, why is you mad at Mr. Mitch?"

The woman gave the child's shoulder a small squeeze. "Phoebe, why don't you go pick up your coloring book and crayons and put them away?"

Phoebe crossed her arms over her chest. "But I want to know why Mr. Mitch made you mad."

"He didn't make me mad, sweetie." The woman bared her teeth in what was probably supposed to be a smile, as if that would put some weight behind her words.

Phoebe tilted her head and pointed. "Then why does you got your mad face on?"

Mitch laughed, just a brief exhale of air, but he tried to cover it up by clearing his throat. With both mother and daughter now staring at him, he squared his shoulders. "Maybe we should start over. I'm Mitch Sawicki and I'm looking for Lieutenant Bowie Griffin."

The woman shook her head. "He's not here. If you'd like to leave your contact information, I can have him get in touch."

Damn. Why hadn't he thought this through? He'd been so driven to get to Sarge that he hadn't given logistics a second thought. What was wrong with his thought process? Normally, he'd never go into a situation without a contingency plan and yet, here he was, standing before strangers with no back-up plan. Had he expected these people to hand over the dog on his say so?

He pushed the doubts aside because he hadn't come all this way to be thwarted now. Besides, relating to a fellow military man had to be easier than dealing with these two. Right? "When are you expecting him? Maybe I can—"

"Mr. Mitch?" Phoebe tugged on his pant leg.

"Sometimes it takes a long time for Uncle Bo to come home when he's off saving the world."

Puzzled by her words, he glanced down and frowned. "Saving the world?"

She'd called Lieutenant Griffin Uncle Bo. That little bit of information didn't escape his notice. Did this mean the woman wasn't Mrs. Bowie Griffin and he wasn't going to be condemned for his lascivious thoughts? Or was *uncle* a child's euphemism for her mother's boyfriend? Those thoughts were best left alone for now. It was something he'd deal with later. If at all.

The girl's head bobbed up and down. "Uh-huh. Saving the world is his job. He—"

"Phoebe," the woman said with a clear note of warning in her tone.

"Oops. I'm not a'spose to talk about that. It's another *rule*." Phoebe dragged out the last word, giving it an extra syllable. She sniffed and her shoulders dropped as if unable to support the weight of her burden.

"Ouch. Sometimes rules can be hard to keep track of, huh?" Mitch said, hoping to diffuse the situation. Tears—no matter the age of the woman in question—had the power to unman him.

Damn, what was wrong with him? Had he totally abandoned his purpose? No, but those solemn eyes gazing up at him had twisted something in his chest. He still hadn't asked about Sarge. How had these two managed to throw him into such chaos?

"I'm sorry I didn't catch your name," he said to

the woman, figuring he'd get this whole episode back onto an even keel and find out where he could locate Sarge. One look at this dog's ear tattoo and he'd have his answer.

"My mommy is Sleeping Beauty," the pint-sized princess announced.

"Excuse me?" Mitch looked from Phoebe to her mother, whose cheeks had turned a deeper shade of pink. Yes, the blush was intriguing, but it was that oh so slight sexy-as-hell overbite that had his insides twisting into knots. How did she and the child fit into this scenario and what was Sarge to them?

"She means my name is Aurora," she explained and shot Phoebe a look that promised retribution.

"Aurora?" Why was he reduced to repeating the last thing she said? He couldn't remember ever feeling so tongue-tied around an attractive woman. Perhaps his smooth moves had come easier when both the legs he was standing on were his own.

"Yes, but everyone just calls me Rory."

"Rory," he said, testing it out. He liked it, liked the way it felt on his lips. "But I don't understand—"

"She's *Princess* Aurora," Phoebe said as if that explained everything and gave her mother a look of pure adoration.

"Princess Aurora?" Mitch arched an eyebrow as he studied the woman in front of him. Exactly what sort of rabbit hole had he fallen through?

"Despite Phoebe's claim, it's just Aurora." The woman sighed. "In case you missed the clues, my daughter is obsessed with fairy tales."

"I noticed." Mitch winked at the giggling little girl. "You may have to remind me about the one with Princess Phoebe and her magical red boots."

"Mommy, Mr. Mitch thinks I'm a princess and that my new boots are magic," Phoebe said in an awed stage whisper.

Hoping to ease the sudden tightness, Mitch rubbed his chest. Not having spent any time around kids, he was clueless, but it looked like he was the one who'd been missing out all this time.

Rory Walsh could only nod at Phoebe's comment. She was too busy trying to gulp down a breath. Mitch's wink had been directed at Phoebe, but it had landed on her and done something diabolical to her lungs. But even before that devastating wink, she'd been intrigued by his pale green eyes, so striking against the olive tone of his skin. He had full lips and, as much as she tried not to, she couldn't help but wonder how that mouth would feel against hers.

Despite the unkempt hair that was months past needing to be trimmed, she'd pegged Mitch as military, either current or former. She hadn't come to that conclusion just because he wore fatigues. Anyone could buy those army-green pants and T-shirts at a surplus store or off the internet. She'd been raised by a former marine turned sheriff's deputy, plus her brother was active-duty navy. So, yeah, she recognized that stance...*and* that innate attitude.

"So, you're like a princess in disguise?" Mitch asked, quirking an eyebrow at her.

Rory worked to reconnect with the conversation. Sighing, she silently cursed her blabbermouth daughter. "That was her real name."

Mitch frowned. "Whose real name?"

"Sleeping Beauty," mother and daughter said at the same time.

The poor guy looked totally confused, which somehow added to his appeal. The best thing she could do was send him on his way before she did something stupid like invite him in. Or worse, check to see how those lips felt against hers. When had she gotten so bold? She hadn't even dated since the divorce, let alone engage in any torrid affairs. So why was she suddenly having these surprising, and disturbing, thoughts? And in front of her daughter, no less.

"As I said, if you'd like to leave a number or a message, I'll pass it along to my brother," she said in as brusque a tone as she could manage.

If she hadn't been looking closely, she might have missed the expression of relief on his face when she'd said Bowie was her brother. Interesting.

No. Not interesting. Not nothing. Oh great, now she was bending grammar like Phoebe.

She wrapped her fingers around the edge of the door as if in preparation to shut it. Maybe he'd take the hint and leave and she wouldn't have to deal with these rogue thoughts about him.

"What about the job?"

Chapter Two

"Job?" she repeated lamely. Damn. That's right. She'd asked him if that's why he'd come. Why hadn't she kept her big mouth shut?

She'd posted the notice at the library, figuring a high school kid would respond. Then she could tell Walt that they'd be helping out a needy kid by giving him a job. She'd never be able to convince her uncle they were doing a guy like Mitch a favor by letting him help out on Bowie's farm. Despite his doctor's advice, Walt refused to slow down, feeling it was his duty to keep the farm in top shape while Bowie was off serving his country. Her brother had purchased the farmhouse and acreage on the outskirts of town, so he'd have someplace to call home once his military career was over.

She understood her uncle's pride demanded he

repay Bowie's generosity. Her brother had provided both his uncle and his sister a place to live. She had moved in with Phoebe after her divorce two years ago and finances were tight because she was still paying off her portion of the loans she and her ex-husband had secured to open the restaurant they lost after a fire destroyed the kitchen. They'd been under-insured thanks to her ex.

When her brother learned of her troubles, he'd insisted she and Phoebe move to his farm. Her job at the school cafeteria didn't pay well but at least she could manage a token amount for rent.

Her uncle had followed suit after his place had fallen victim to a wildfire and he'd run into obstacles in rebuilding. He'd retired as a sheriff's deputy with a full twenty years on the job after his heart attack.

She felt the same way as Walt about accepting handouts, but they also had to face reality. Walt was financially stable but struggling physically to keep up with everything that needed doing on the farm.

Bowie had started sending money to hire someone.

Hiring someone else was the only solution she could think of to ease Walt's current workload. Walt had been there for her and her brother when their parents had been killed by a couple of careless teens drag racing on a public road. She and Bowie wanted to be there for him now.

Walt hadn't hesitated to take in two grief-stricken teens and raise them as if they'd been his own. He'd given them love and unconditional support, allowing each one to heal at their own pace, in their own way, but providing professional help when necessary.

Now, they wanted to be there for him. Some might call it an obligation but they didn't see it that way and were happy to help.

"Mommy? Is you going to hire Mr. Mitch?" Phoebe clapped her hands and bounced on her toes.

"What?" Phoebe's question snapped Rory back to the here and now. "Absolutely not. I—"

"You're dismissing me without so much as an interview?" Mitch huffed out a puff of air through his lips. "That's rather hasty, isn't it?"

"Mr. Mitch? I don't know what *hasty* means," Phoebe said in a petulant tone, her gaze ping-ponging between the adults.

"It means your mom doesn't want to give me a chance to interview for the job." Mitch's pale eyes held a challenging gleam.

Great. If she actually expressed how attracted to him she was, she'd probably be in violation of all sorts of labor laws. Rory narrowed her eyes, saying, "I thought you came here looking for my brother. Not a job."

He couldn't be serious about wanting employment. Or could he? She studied him a bit more closely. Despite his messy hair, Mitch did not look like he was down on his luck—needing an hourly job doing manual labor for her. For all she knew that shaggy hair could be some sort of fashion statement. She knew all about those, she thought dryly, casting a glance at Phoebe's rain boots and crown.

"Well, now that I'm here, I'd like to hear more about this job." He ran the fingers of one hand through his hair, messing it up even more.

Would all those ebony strands be as silky as they looked? And since when was messy hair so sexy?

"Mommy, I think you should hire Mr. Mitch. I like him."

"Looks like I have your daughter's endorsement," he said with a lopsided lift of his lips.

Damn him and that crooked smile. She'd bet it could charm the pants off any woman he met. "I don't take hiring advice from a three-year-old."

"But, Mommy, I'm four now. Did you forget my birthday? Did you forget I'm four now?"

Why was she feeling like this was two against one all of a sudden? "No, sweetie, I haven't forgotten. I just think Mr. Mitch is probably overqualified for this job."

One dark eyebrow quirked up. "And you would know this how? You haven't even asked for my résumé. Or checked my qualifications."

She met his gaze and the challenge lurking in those depths. "Résumé? You can't be serious."

"Why can't I be serious?"

"First off, it's only part-time and the pay is really crappy." It was the truth but what if he was a friend of Bo's? He could be down on his luck and need whatever work he could get. Maybe she shouldn't be so quick to dismiss him. Walt wouldn't turn his back on a fellow vet. Nor would Bo. And she wouldn't either.

But did she want to be around someone as tempting as him on a daily basis? She had no place in her life for a man. She was still getting used to life after a divorce. Despite the fact she and Curt remained on cordial terms for Phoebe's sake, the divorce had stung. She hated failing. The failed business had been the first strike, the divorce strike two. She wasn't going for a third possible failure.

Nor was she going to put Phoebe through having someone yanked from her daily life again. Her duty was to her daughter. While Phoebe seemed well-adjusted and content, Rory knew her child hadn't escaped unscathed from the divorce, even though it had been conducted in a polite and civil manner. She hadn't come through unscathed; how could she expect that her daughter had?

"I think you might be going about this all wrong. The crappier the job the more you should be selling it. I don't know exactly what this job entails but you should be touting its benefits. For example, how it involves such fun coworkers like Phoebe here," he said and winked at Phoebe, who giggled.

"I want to be a coworker, Mommy. Can I? Please. I'll be a good coworker. I promise."

Rory heaved an exasperated sigh. How had this gotten so out of hand? "Phoebe, I'm *not* going to ask you again to go and pick up your crayons."

"But, Mommy, I—"

"No buts. Now." She turned Phoebe around and

prodded her gently in the small of her back. She had enough dealing with her surprise visitor, she didn't need the added distraction of her daughter. After making sure Phoebe had gone into the kitchen to clean up the mess, she turned back to Mitch.

Those lips looked pinched at the moment, and she noticed he was rubbing his thigh again. He'd already done so several times during the conversation. Was he in pain or was it an unconscious gesture, like a nervous tic?

"Are you okay? Do you need to sit or something?" She started to reach out but dropped her hand when he jerked back as if she'd been going to strike him.

"What makes you ask that?" he asked in a chilly tone.

"I noticed you were rubbing your leg." She shrugged, unwilling to confess her attraction to him in order to explain why she was taking such an interest in his movements. "I guess it's the mother in me."

Color stained his cheeks and those gorgeous green eyes turned flat. "I already have a mother. I don't need another."

Well...okay. Now it was her turn to blush. Parenting was the last thing she had in mind for him. That thought had nervous laughter bubbling up and she had to quash it because she didn't want to laugh if he was in pain. Instead, she was tempted to tell him that he needed to leave. Like right now. Before she let something slip.

Sure, her reaction to him was irrational, but that was the definition of an irrational fear. Her fear didn't stem from feeling as though she was in physical danger. No, the danger stemmed from the fact that she couldn't stop wondering what his lips would feel like on hers every time he opened that sexy mouth. And because she wasn't looking to move on romantically at this point in time, this conversation had to end. Now.

"As I said, if you want to leave your information with me, I will have my brother contact you." The need to nip this conversation in the bud took precedence over her distracting thoughts before she did something even more stupid. Like hire him.

"So you won't even consider me?"

Oh, she'd consider him. That's why she didn't want him here. She could too easily imagine him shirtless, his chest covered in sweat, swinging an ax.

An ax? Really? Stop this right now. It was springtime cool, and they had no need for—

"So, I take that as a no?"

The sound of his voice penetrated her fugue and the pictures in her head of a shirtless Mitch evaporated like a puff of smoke in a brisk wind.

"Grandpa G and Sarge are home." Phoebe burst through the open doorway onto the porch.

Rory grabbed her daughter's shoulder to halt her progress. "Phoebe, what have I told you about leaving the porch when there's a car coming?"

"But—but..." Phoebe sputtered and pointed to

the thirty-year-old pickup heading down the drive-way. "I want Mr. Mitch to meet my doggy."

"Mr. Sawicki can hardly miss that dog since he's standing right here."

"Sarge is the best dog in the whole wide world. He made me not so sad when my daddy couldn't live with us no more." Phoebe looked at their visi-tor. "He was gonna belong to my uncle Bo but Sarge and I love each other the mostest, so he said Sarge could be mine. Forever and ever."

A red Dodge Ram was making its way down the long drive, its rear wheels kicking up dust and pebbles in its wake. Mitch tore his gaze away from the older-model truck and looked at the little girl. Her words regarding Sarge scraping his insides with what felt like a hot poker.

His stomach dropped to the vicinity of his knees. What the hell was he supposed to do? Walk away? Pray that this dog wasn't *his* Sarge? He prayed his dog had survived, but if he had, what would that mean? How could he lay claim to this innocent child's pet?

"Where did your uncle get the dog?" he asked in what he'd hoped was a conversational tone, but he sensed Rory tensing. Did she suspect him of hav-ing a nefarious reason for asking about the canine?

"He 'dopted him from the army when the man who hads him couldn't take care of him no more. Isn't that right, Mommy?"

Her gaze still trained on him, Rory nodded to

her daughter. Mitch bit back the automatic denial that sprang up. How dare anyone say he couldn't look after his K9 partner?

But you know it was true at the time, a voice in his head taunted.

He'd been in a morphine-induced haze while the pararescue jumpers risked their own lives to evacuate wounded from the blast site that had morphed into a battle zone. Despite being pumped full of drugs, he'd grabbed the arm of one of the PJs and asked about Sarge. Mitch could vividly recall how the man's already worn expression had fallen further. His comrade had resignedly shaken his head and whispered in a low, sad voice, "Sorry." After that, Mitch had let the darkness swallow him whole, even relished the numbing blankness. From his short stint in Germany to being brought back to Walter Reed in Virginia, the days and weeks had merged together.

His heartbeat kicked up and he wiped his sweaty palms on his pant legs as the dusty pickup drew closer. This was the moment of truth. He'd find out if Sarge had survived the blast that had stolen so much from him. Had the other soldier lied? Been mistaken? Had Mitch been so out of it that he had misheard that one word?

Did Sarge—if this was indeed his former partner—think Mitch had simply abandoned him? That thought was like a fist squeezing his gut. Sarge had had to go through losing *his* leg without Mitch's support. The fist tightened.

How many times had Sarge alerted him to explosives, saving not only Mitch's life but others as well? For Sarge to have put himself in danger in order to protect Mitch intensified his guilt over what could be perceived as abandonment. He should have done more. Why had he taken someone else's word that Sarge hadn't made it?

He glanced at Phoebe who was balancing on her toes waiting for her dog.

And what happens if this is your Sarge? an insidious voice asked as the truck pulled up with a majestic, black-masked dog peering out of the passenger window. Mitch recognized Sarge's rich mahogany coloring and black tipped ears. Mitch was too far away to see the tattoo in the dog's ear for confirmation of his identity.

The dog barked. Was that bark for him or for Phoebe?

Could he simply walk away even if this was his former partner? What other choice did he have if it meant breaking a little girl's heart?

"Can I go now?" Phoebe asked as the truck came to a stop and its engine sputtered to a halt.

"Wait for Grandpa G to get out," Rory instructed.

Phoebe looked up at Mitch, her dark-eyed gaze catching his. "It's another ru-ule."

"We have these rules because I'm trying to keep you safe, young lady," her mother informed her.

Phoebe heaved an exasperated sigh. "I bet you don't have a bunch of rules, do you, Mr. Mitch?"

He thought of the list of precautions he'd been

given upon his discharge from the hospital. They'd told him the instructions were designed to prevent skin infections and other problems caused by his prosthetic. "Believe it or not, Princess, I have an entire list of them. And I've been told they're for my own good."

Those instructions might be beneficial but, like Phoebe, he sometimes felt frustrated by the restrictions, the changes to his daily life.

"But you's an adult." Her wide eyes narrowed with suspicion. "Is you just saying that?"

He held up his hand as if taking an oath. His face transformed into a mask of sincerity. "I swear it's the truth."

Before she could demand an explanation, the older man who'd been driving the truck exited and slammed his door shut.

"Can I go now?" Phoebe pleaded.

"You may." Rory smiled indulgently at her daughter and turned to him with that smile still in place. "You'd think they'd been separated for months instead of a couple hours."

Even as that smile did strange things to his gut, her words stung like shrapnel.

The little girl raced off the porch. "Grandpa G, Grandpa G, guess what? Mr. Mitch is here. I answered the door and there he was. He wants to meet my doggy."

"Is that so? And what does Mr. Mitch want with us?" Walt Griffin patted his granddaughter's head.

"Mommy is going to give him a job."

"A what?" Walt had been reaching for the door handle but dropped his hand and looked to the porch.

Mitch heard the conversation, but his attention was on the dog wriggling in the passenger seat. He sure looked like *his* Sarge.

The barks became frantic, and he clawed at the window to get out.

The older man reached up and opened the passenger door and the animal burst out of the truck.

"Mitch, I need to tell—" Rory began but what she was going to say was lost in a flurry of excited barking.

The dog had stumbled when he hit the ground but scrambled up, barely missing a beat. Sarge whimpered with excitement, licking Phoebe's face when she ran forward and threw her arms around his neck. The dog pulled his little mistress along with him as he tried to get to Mitch.

Mitch tensed as an alarming rush of emotions bubbled up. Three legs. He had known from the video that this Sarge had only three legs but knowing and seeing were two different things. The dog's left front leg was gone in an almost bizarre copy of Mitch's injuries. Damn. Guilt lanced through him. He hated that his partner had gone through that without him. Guilt, excitement, and relief threatened to overwhelm him forcing Mitch to shut down his emotions. He needed to concentrate on getting through the next few minutes without breaking down and bawling in front of these three strangers. Despite not checking the tattoo yet, he knew in his heart this was his former companion.

Spreading his arms, he hunkered down. Sarge leaped at him, knocking him on his butt. Mitch chuckled and rubbed the dog's head while checking the ear tattoo. A108. Bingo. His hunch had paid off and he'd located his K9 companion. Now, the task was to get him back where he belonged.

He made me not so sad... Sarge and I love each other the mostest... The innocent young girl's comments bombarded him and that sick feeling in his stomach returned. Could he somehow deprive a lonely little girl of a much-needed furry friend? Though he did wonder what in Rory and Phoebe's lives made them so sad... He hadn't noticed a ring on Rory's slender finger. Was Phoebe's dad—or a father figure—even in the picture? That might mean her beautiful mother was single... Mitch shook his head violently to rid himself of the unwelcome—or all *too* welcome—thoughts and turned back to the newcomers.

"Uncle Walt, this is Mitch Sawicki. Mitch, this is my uncle, Walter Griffin," said Rory.

Mitch found his footing and rose, albeit unsteadily, but kept on rubbing Sarge's head.

"Pleasure to meet you, sir." Mitch thrust out his free hand. He wondered why Phoebe had referred to him as her grandfather but didn't ask. None of his business. And he had no plans to make any of this family's relationships his business. He was here for Sarge—no one else, whether they were dog or human.

"What branch were you in?" Walt shook his hand. He grinned, probably from Mitch's reaction, and added, "You got that look about you, son."

Mitch raised an eyebrow. "Takes one to know one, sir."

"That it does." Walt nodded. "Me, I put my full twenty into the corps."

"I was army but didn't serve quite that many." This wasn't the time for explanation why he didn't make it as long as he'd planned. Looking for sympathy seemed underhanded when he'd come seeking to regain ownership of Sarge. If not for Phoebe and her earnest declaration of love for the dog, he would have pressed his case. Now… How could he do that to a child? Mitch felt lost and at his wits' end. This whole journey had been his focus ever since he'd first heard of this dog. If he wasn't able to rescue Sarge, then what would he do now?

For that short time, he'd had a purpose, a goal to achieve. If he lost that, what did he have?

Chapter Three

Trying to regain Mitch's attention, Sarge pressed up against his former partner and made a noise in his throat. Mitch laughed and vigorously rubbed the soft fur between his ears. "I'm right here, bud."

"I gotta say I've never seen him react that way to meeting someone new. He's not unfriendly but more reserved than this. It's..." Walt Griffin trailed off and rubbed his chin. "It's almost as if he knows you."

"Well, I..." Mitch swallowed back the snarled tangle of emotions that kept threatening to overwhelm him. Finding the dog alive was joyous for sure and, while it hurt Mitch to see the empty spot where a leg should be, Sarge appeared unhampered by his missing limb. Not to mention he wasn't sure he'd be able to reunite with his K9 after all— He had to push those thoughts aside or risk embarrassing himself by turning into a blubbering mess. He cleared his throat.

"I worked with dogs when I was in the army," Mitch offered, hoping the succinct explanation would satisfy them. At least for now.

"He likes you, Mr. Mitch," Phoebe said and threw her arms around a wriggling Sarge. "He's just the best dog ever and I love him so much."

"Still kinda odd," Walt said as he continued to watch the dog interact with Mitch.

It was obvious that Walt suspected something. Was he keeping his suspicions to himself in front of Phoebe? Mitch hoped that was the case because he didn't want to tell outright lies to the older man, but he also wasn't prepared to discuss the dog's ownership in front of Phoebe either.

Mitch didn't stand a chance in an ownership dispute because when Sarge was his partner, the dog belonged to the army not to his handler. Which showed him how rash his decision to come here had been.

Oblivious to the sudden tension between the two male adults, Phoebe balanced on her toes. "Guess what, Grandpa G? Mr. Mitch is going to work here and I'm going to be a coworker."

"Work?" Walt frowned. He turned to Rory. "What's this about hiring someone? Do you mean to work here? On the farm? What the heck would he even do? I don't see any need for—"

"I think there's been some confusion," Rory in-

terrupted, that appealing furrow crossing her otherwise smooth brow again. "Phoebe, did you pick
up your crayons like I asked?"

"Uh-huh. I already done that. I put them all back
in the box." She put her hands on her hips. "And
you said I could be a coworker for Mr. Mitch. You
said so, Mommy."

"Phoebe, I didn't—"

"Why would you be hiring someone?" Walt
scowled, his gaze darting between Rory and Mitch.

Mitch had the urge to throw up his hands, palms
out, in a gesture of innocence, but he didn't. His
presence here had started all of this. That didn't
make him guilty, but he understood both sides. It
sounded as if Rory genuinely wanted to help her
uncle, and the former marine's pride was on the
line if his abilities were in question. Didn't Mitch
himself decide to leave the army when he couldn't
perform in his previous capacity?

Rory had that deer in the headlights look. "Well,
I—"

"Grandpa G, Mommy said you can't do all
the stuffs on the farm anymore since your heart
attacked-ed you."

Mitch clamped his lips shut over the chuckle that
wanted to escape. He should be annoyed at these
strangers making decisions that affected his life
but he was more amused by their family interac-
tions than upset. Sarge was in the care of people
with genuine affection for one another despite hav-

ing differences of opinion. He had no idea why that mattered so much but it did.

"Says who?" Walt crossed his arms over his chest. "You know as well as I do that the doctors said regular exercise is important. And Lord knows, you won't let me eat anything remotely enjoyable anymore."

Rory shook her head. "That's not what this is about."

"But, Mommy, I heard you tell Mrs. Addie at the liberry that's why you wanted to put up that paper on her bulletin board."

Rory briefly closed her eyes. "Phoebe, please."

Walt rounded on Rory. "Do you mean to tell me that you're blabbing all over town that I'm not capable of taking care of this place anymore?"

"Of course not. I just… I just…"

Mitch understood Walt's bruised ego. His had been wounded from his ex at a time when he'd been vulnerable. *Don't think about any of that now*, he ordered himself.

Still grappling with his emotions threatening to erupt, he had to clear his throat before plunging in. Why was he even doing this? Was it empathy for a fellow veteran or something more? Something he didn't want to examine now…if ever. Nevertheless, he decided to plunge in. "You'd actually be helping me out, sir."

This might be an innocuous lie but he had a feeling it might come back to haunt him at some point.

They all turned to him and his hand automatically reached out to rub one of Sarge's ears. Hmm... maybe Phoebe knew what she was talking about when she said she found Sarge's presence comforting. But that wasn't anything new. The dog had been more than just a four-legged partner to him. Only now he didn't even have— *No! Don't go there.*

"Helping you?" Walt narrowed his eyes and made a *harrumph* sound. "How you figure that, son?"

"Your nephew did me a solid and I would very much like to return the favor." Mitch figured all that was technically true. He didn't know Bowie Griffin, but the man had taken in Sarge and given him a home, despite the dog's handicap. And Mitch had worked closely with Sarge for long enough that he could tell Sarge was happy here, on the Griffins' family farm.

As much as it hurt to admit it, Sarge was probably doing a better job than Mitch of adjusting to the loss of his leg. Of course, Sarge had a caring family to help. Mitch winced. That wasn't true. He had his mother, a very caring woman, but after a week of her smothering attention and crying when she thought he couldn't hear, he decided he was better off alone. So he'd told her he needed to report back to Fort Bragg and packed up his belongings and drove back to the base. Frankly, it had frightened him to see the strong woman who'd raised him on her own fall apart. He'd been barely keeping himself together.

Before his injuries he'd been supremely confident in his abilities. Afterwards, he was forced to face the fact he'd used that confidence as a sort of armor, something between himself and others.

"Tell me, young man," Walt looked Mitch up and down, "how does working here accomplish that?"

"Mommy, why is Grandpa G mad at Mr. Mitch? I don't know why everyone is getting mad at him. Sarge and I like Mr. Mitch," she said and pushed her bottom lip out.

Mitch suppressed the grin Phoebe's expression caused. He understood the other man's reluctance, but he wasn't about to let that understanding lead to a confession. Not yet.

"Phoebe, why don't you go inside and let the grownups talk," Rory suggested.

"But—"

Rory cut off her protests with, "You can take Sarge with you and give him a biscuit. Just one."

"O-kay," Phoebe said, drawing out the word. "But what if he wants two?"

"Then you tell him I said one. Remember Dr. Greer said how important it is for Sarge to maintain a healthy weight because he's carrying those pounds around on three legs."

Sarge whined as if he'd understood the exchange and pressed closer to Mitch. The dog's reaction tugged at his insides. He wished he could reassure the dog—and himself—that things would work out but he couldn't.

"Better go inside with Phoebe. I don't have any treats and one is better than none," Mitch told the dog, even though he was as reluctant to be parted so soon after finding one another.

Sarge and Phoebe made their way up the porch steps. Mitch suspected their slow progress had more to do with reluctance to go inside than Sarge's missing limb. He could sympathize with both girl and canine.

"Go," Mitch said when the dog looked back, and, although he whined Sarge obeyed.

Walt scowled at that. "Are you sure that—"

"You're right. It's more than just wanting to pay your nephew back..." Mitch began and waited until Phoebe and Sarge disappeared into the house. "I could use a hand getting back on my feet after mustering out."

Walt glanced at Mitch's classic blue and white Toyota FJ Cruiser. Despite clearly being used, the SUV was in pristine condition. The original owner had been a fellow Ranger who hadn't made it home. When Bobby Garon's widow had contacted Mitch asking if he was interested in Garon's beloved FJ Cruiser, Mitch had not only jumped at the opportunity but made sure he gave her more cash than necessary. The way he figured it, that combat pay he'd earned was well spent helping a widow and her three kids. Plus, he'd honor his friend by loving the vehicle. It wasn't as if he'd be needing that money for a honeymoon or a down payment on a home. There'd be no wedding, no honeymoon, no house to fill with kids. He wasn't sure he had the strength to put himself out there like that again. A reaction he couldn't have imagined before this. That explosion had shattered more than his leg. And the FJ Cruiser at least *looked* as though it fit the active person he used to be and was working toward being again.

Before the older man could say anything more, Mitch said, "I'm not talking about money or looking for a handout, I just need some direction for the future. I need to feel a part of something again. Helping Griffin's family could do that."

Mitch had said it to distract Walt but now that the words were out, he realized the sentiment behind them was true. For the first time in a long time, he didn't have his future all planned out. He needed to prove himself as a civilian...not just to others but to himself. And if his hunch about this Bo Griffin being Special Forces was correct, they'd have no way to contact him to dispute his story. Mitch figured by the time Bo returned, the situation would have resolved itself. One way or another.

Walt nodded. "I had Rory and her brother to keep me occupied after I left, but I can understand the sentiment."

Mitch gave them a quizzical glance but didn't say anything. *Remember you're not getting involved.*

"Uncle Walt gave Bowie and me a home after our parents were killed in a car accident," Rory answered Mitch's unspoken question.

Mitch flinched at her quietly spoken words. Her sharing of such an intimate detail made him regret his own lack of candor. And it made him admire her, a feeling that went deeper than appreciating her looks.

"I'm sorry for your loss. How old were you?" he asked, not wanting to ignore her comment.

"I was twelve and Bowie was fifteen. Walt gave up his carefree, bachelor lifestyle for us."

"Wasn't much of a sacrifice." Walt chuckled, but with the look he gave Rory, the gruff marine disappeared, replaced by a sentimental middle-aged man.

The affection between them was obvious and Mitch felt as though he were witnessing a private family moment. He should give his mother a call. She might have a tendency to smother, but she was the only mother he had and he was her only child. Guilt at his hasty departure prodded him. But that was what had made him such a good army recruit—he was order over emotion, every time. A cavernous hole suddenly gaped in front of him. What was he going to do with his life now that he no longer had that institution, that structure, driving his every action?

Walt turned to Mitch. "What was it you were planning to do to help around here?"

Mitch felt exposed, as if Walt could see through the ruse. He hated to lie to the former marine, but he had no idea what kind of job Rory had in mind. He could assume that it had to do with the farm but the last time he made an assumption, he was confronted with a miniature princess instead of what he'd been expecting.

"We hadn't gotten that far...yet," Rory said, looking at him as if afraid of what he might say. As if she was worried he might reject the tenuous job offer. *Does she want me to stay?* he wondered. Not that he'd mind spending more time around a beautiful woman, especially if she was his dog's current owner.

"She was telling me about the long hours and the crappy pay...really selling me on the job," Mitch joked.

"So, she was telling the truth." Walt stroked his chin. "Rory, honey, I think you need to work on your sales technique."

"Frankly, I think she was trying to discourage me," Mitch said and gave her a pointed look to indicate his determination.

"And yet you're still here." Rory crossed her arms.

"I don't scare easily, and a little hard work doesn't bother me." That was the truth, but the way he felt about her and the look she was giving him made him a bit uneasy. He couldn't help but wonder what it would feel like to put his lips against hers and kiss that cross look off her face.

"You say you were army?" Walt asked.

"Yes, sir."

"That explains a lot. But I guess I won't hold that against you."

"Walt," Rory said in a scolding tone.

"We marines had to finish the job."

"You guys brought up the rear because Rangers lead the way." Mitch had spotted the teasing twinkle in the older man's eyes and didn't mind pulling the man's chain. He appreciated his brothers in arms, regardless of the branches they served in. And he was sure Walt did too. Of course that wasn't something they'd readily admit to one another.

Walt snorted. "If that's what you want to tell yourself."

"Walt, please, no insults," Rory said and sighed.

"What? He's a Ranger, he can take it." Walt put an arm around her shoulder and hugged her. "You were the one trying to run him off by describing this supposed job."

"I was just being honest," she said. "And there is nothing *supposed* about it."

Mitch was surprised at how quickly he'd grown to enjoy the Griffin family's genial banter. He wished he had those types of close bonds with his own relatives …or his ex-fiancée.

Walt grunted. "I ain't ready to be put out to pasture yet."

She kissed his whiskered cheek. "I couldn't turn a friend of Bowie's away."

Walt grunted and dropped his arm. "Well, Army, do you know anything about building a greenhouse or a coop? She's got it in her head she wants chickens."

"In the past, I've done volunteer work with organizations like Habitat for Humanity and picked up rudimentary skills. The structure might not be an architectural work of art but it would be sturdy," Mitch said.

"Well, there you go," Walt said with a motion of his hand.

She tutted her tongue. "Uncle Walt, if Mitch stays, I think *he* should be helping *you*."

Mitch noticed she spoke as if his staying wasn't a foregone conclusion. He would have said the same thing about fifteen minutes ago, but suddenly he wanted to stay. Because of Sarge, of course, he reasoned to himself. It had nothing to do with the warmth emanating from the Griffin household that threatened to overwhelm him or even thaw his heart. Or Rory's sparkling eyes or the way she smelled of orange blossoms. Or the sweet little girl in red rain boots and tinfoil crown. Or the retired marine who might or might not need or even want help. Nope. None of that.

Rory noticed that Mitch didn't seem offended by Walt's comments regarding his choice of military branch. In fact, the slight crinkle in the crow's feet by his eyes indicated that both he and Walt got a kick out of it. When Walt and Ogle Whatley, another army vet, got together the supposed insults would fly. Each claiming their branch of the service ruled.

"Building you a greenhouse would be helping me by freeing me up," Walt said.

"I don't need—"

"Yes, you do," Walt said, nodding his head. "How else are you going to get this farm-to-table idea of yours off the ground? I've been doing some research on what it takes to supply restaurants with local vegetables and those herbs and edible flowers you're wanting to grow. Although why anyone would want to eat flowers is beyond me."

"You've been doing research?"

"I'm not the old fuddy-duddy you and your brother seem to think I am. I know how to use the internet the same as you."

"Uncle Walt! We don't think that."

Walt waved her protests away. "So, Mitch, can you construct a greenhouse?"

"Looks like we're going to find out," Mitch said and chuckled.

"I'm going to leave you two to sort this out. I'll be in the house making sure Munchkin doesn't give that dog too many biscuits." Walt went into the house.

Rory nodded, not trusting her voice. Her insides had melted at the resonance of that chuckling sound from Mitch. She sneaked a peek at him and swallowed, twice, fearing she might start drooling. He was definitely a glorious specimen of a man. It was enough to almost make her forget her vow that she was off men. Keyword being *almost*. Her failed relationship still stung. She didn't want to put Phoebe through anything like that again. Given time, she'd think up a few more excuses.

What was wrong with her? She'd only just met this guy and she was thinking about relationships? She'd failed to make things work with Phoebe's father. She and Curt had married because she'd gotten pregnant, but the strain of their failed business had taken its toll on the relationship. Curt might be a wonderfully inventive chef but a businessman he was not. Even before the fire that had destroyed their restaurant, they'd struggled financially.

In hindsight she took equal responsibility because she'd taken Curt's word for it that he'd renewed the insurance. He hadn't and the fire ruined the restaurant…and eventually the marriage. "…more about this farm-to-table thing."

She blinked, heat rushing to her cheeks. "I'm sorry. What did you say?"

"I said I'd like to learn more about this farm-to-table thing."

"Right now, it's more aspirational than real. I'm working on being certified organic and hoping to turn it into a full-time business. I've been growing herbs and vegetables that I have sold to local restaurants. I'm hoping to increase my output and branch into some new items."

"Like edible flowers?" Mitch asked with a quirk of a dark eyebrow.

She laughed. "Yeah, those too."

"And the chickens? Are you going to provide them with meat?"

"I've been thinking about providing them with fresh local eggs. One of the many classes I have taken through the county extension service has been on raising chickens for egg production. Mary Wilson offered to sell me most of her chickens, but I need to be able to house them safely first."

Rory knew Mary didn't have time to devote to

her chickens or egg gathering with her growing family and thriving nonprofit. Mary and her husband, Brody, offered underprivileged children an opportunity to experience summer camp at their farm. Rory could only hope to be half as successful as the Wilsons with her growing business venture. Her dream was simple. She wanted to provide a home for Phoebe and get out from under the financial burden her ex-husband's actions had created. The restaurant may have closed but the business loans remained and they shared the financial burden despite the divorce, each making monthly payments.

Curt wasn't a bad person and despite not having a fulltime role in Phoebe's daily life, he was a loving father and was always on time with his child support payments. Good thing too because her income felt like a cobbled together affair with her job at the school cafeteria and what little she made from the current farm to table business.

"Do you have plans for the coop and greenhouse?"

Mitch's question snapped her back to their current circumstances and she frowned. "Isn't that what I was just talking about?"

He raised an eyebrow at her sharp tone. "I meant blueprint-type plans."

"Oh," she muttered, heat still warming her cheeks. He'd hit a nerve. She didn't trust herself to make a go of this. One failed business along with a failed marriage made her doubt herself. But she

had to at least try. She owed that much to Phoebe—
and, if she were honest, to herself. If she wanted her
daughter to grow up confident, she needed to parent by example. Which is why she was doing her
best to maintain a friendly relationship with her ex
and because they shared custody. "I don't have professional ones, like from an architect or anything."

"I'd be surprised if you had."

What was that supposed to mean? Was he paying her back for wounded pride when she'd made
that blunder about trying to mother him? "I don't
have the entire operation up and running yet," she
said defensively. She didn't appreciate anyone, especially a man she barely knew, doubting her ambi-
tions without offering a constructive solution.

He held up his hands in the universal sign of sur-
render. "I meant that I wouldn't have expected you
to have hired an architect to design a greenhouse
or a henhouse."

"But I have a file on my laptop with lots of pictures of what I want. Will that help?" Embarrassed
by her lack of business finesse.

"Perfect." He smiled and winked. "I'm not sure
I would know how to read architectural plans anyway."

That sexy, crooked grin increased the heat in her
cheeks. He might annoy her, and she couldn't deny
the attraction, but she *could* choose to ignore it.
Couldn't she? "Great. I have an office in the barn.
I'll show you."

She stepped off the porch, heading toward the

barn. He fell into step beside her and she caught a whiff of citrus, peppery ginger and cedar. Damn but he even smelled good. "You know, I'm not sure I ever actually said I would hire you."

"How can you not? I'm an honorably discharged veteran and your daughter and your dog like me." He widened his smile. "Even your uncle likes me."

She shot him a skeptical glance and he laughed.

"Hey, he's on his way to liking me," he amended. Glancing back toward the house, he said, "And I don't see people lining up for a chance at this amazing employment opportunity."

"As long as you understand I did this to help Walt. He doesn't like to admit any weakness, but I worry about him after last year's heart attack." She understood her uncle's feelings. After all, she hadn't wanted to take a handout from Bowie but Phoebe took precedent, so she swallowed her pride and had accepted her brother's offer of somewhere to live when she couldn't afford the rent on her place. Here, the amount she paid her brother was mostly symbolic. But if she was going to be living with her family once again, then she was determined to make her own way financially. And that meant expanding her business in ways she'd always dreamt of—and ways that would bring in some income.

"Gotcha. Preserve his dignity." He placed his hands on his hips. "But what about mine?"

She frowned in confusion. "Your what?"

"My dignity. For instance, what's my job title?"

"Oh, I'm sure I can think of something. But

that's for tomorrow. You might not appreciate what I might come up with right now," she said and realized she was enjoying the easy back-and-forth. She hadn't had this much fun just chatting with a guy... since, well, long before her relationship with Curt had begun to circle the drain.

"That's what I'm afraid of," he said but chuckled as if he too were enjoying this. Her pulse raced at the low, throaty sound.

They'd reached the barn and she threw open one of the large double doors. Owning this farm had been Bowie's dream. She hadn't understood why he loved this place until she'd come here to live. Something about the place had helped heal her wounded soul. She wondered if Mitch's soul was wounded too. Perhaps being here—*working here*, she amended silently—could help him find whatever he was looking for.

Chapter Four

They didn't currently have any livestock, but the barn had somehow retained the scent of horses, its past occupants. She led him across the cement floor to the small office she'd claimed as her own.

In the office, she booted up her computer and found the images she was looking for. She explained about the greenhouse. "I'm hoping to eventually get to the point where I'm not dependent on the weather."

"Well, it is Vermont."

"True, but the endless rain and storms we had that brought down trees also wreaked havoc on my lavender. I'd been hoping to grow some culinary lavender. Nothing major. Just a small crop but they don't like wet feet, so I need to keep them in a greenhouse while getting them established."

"Wet feet?" He reached for the mouse. "May I?"

"Of course." She pulled her hand away.

"You mentioned something about wet feet?"

"Oh, the lavender. The roots prefer drier soil." Oh God, why was she babbling about lavender roots? Mitch was one of the hottest guys she'd interacted with in a long, long time. At least one that wasn't married or madly in love with— Oh God! Was Mitch married or involved? "Are you married?"

He paused scrolling through her pictures. "What?"

She winced. What was it about this guy that messed with her filter? "I—I, um, just wondered if you were trying to…uh, support a family or anything."

He shook his head. "No kids. No wife or girlfriend."

She swallowed and tried to ignore the sense of relief that flooded her at his reply. "That's good."

He raised an eyebrow and she didn't respond, instead just rushing on. "I mean I…uh, don't have to feel guilty about the low wages."

"As I said, I'm not here looking for a handout." He pointed to the computer screen. "These don't look too complicated. What about the…henhouse? Is there one design you like better than the rest?"

She leaned closer to touch the screen. "This one, but I knew it was beyond anything Walt and I could accomplish so don't feel you have to—"

"I have an idea that might work," he said and scratched his chin. "What about this one?"

"That's a potting shed."

"There's a difference?" he asked.

"Yes, but a potting shed like that one is just one of those maybe someday dreams. It would be a fun luxury more than a necessity."

"Maybe today should be someday."

"I think we'll have enough with the chicken run and henhouse."

"A chicken run?" he asked.

"Yeah, it's not just a decades old Claymation movie," she said and scolded herself for babbling. She went on to explain, "The coop is the interior space and the run is the enclosed exterior space."

He nodded and jotted down some information on the small pad he'd produced from his pocket. He was already thinking about their future—*her future*, she reminded herself sternly. Mitch would help out with the beginnings of her new expansion, but then he would be long gone by the time it came to fruition. As he continued writing, Rory tried to ignore the pang in her heart that thought caused.

She barely knew the man and had no business building castles in the air when it came to she and Mitch. He'd probably be appalled and embarrassed if he could read her thoughts.

Mitch awoke with a start. Where was he? Had they transferred him to a new hospital? Or *facility,* as all the medical professionals liked to call them. As if that made a difference. No matter what the centers were referred to, they all had the same feel-

ing, same airless, disinfectant smell, complete with
the sounds of beeping monitors and hushed voices.
And they all meant that his life had changed. The
way he'd lived before was gone and never coming back.

He needed to take a page out of Sarge's book of
life. The dog seemed happy to be alive—regardless
of how and who he was living with now.

That last thought reminded him this wasn't a
hospital or rehab facility, but a motel on the outskirts of Loon Lake. He sat up and glanced around
the room. The drapes didn't quite meet in the mid-
dle, letting outside light flow in. The place was
exactly as it seemed last night when he'd checked
in. A roadside spot caught in a bit of a time warp,
reminiscent of the motels from a bygone era before the national chains started popping up, even in
small towns like this one. The room boasted utili-
tarian pressboard furniture, brown tweed carpet,
ugly orange drapes and matching bed covers. The
one thing it had going in its favor was that it was
scrupulously clean. He glanced at the bedside clock.
Barely six.

Now, fully awake, all of yesterday's events came
back to him. He'd driven to Vermont from North
Carolina to get Sarge back.

"Yeah, and that went so well," he muttered to
himself as he reached for the gel liner and prosthetic socks he'd set on the nightstand so they'd be
within easy reach in the morning.

Following the doctor's advice, he had taken to

showering at night because the hot water can cause the limb to swell, making it difficult to put on the prosthesis. Although enough time may have passed, making this unnecessary but he'd gotten into the habit and had continued. He'd been telling Phoebe the truth about having a list of do's and don'ts or as she would call them, *ru-ules*, dragging out the word. Against his better judgment, he was finding himself warming to the little girl—and to her mother.

After fitting the gel liner and one of the socks, he reached for the prosthetic. He had left it propped against one of the nightstands that were bolted to the wall on either side of the bed. He needed to put it on before rising; otherwise the blood could pool and the socket wouldn't fit correctly. He could add more socks if the fit was too loose but there wasn't a lot he could do if it was too tight. A number of things could cause the stump to swell.

Stump. He turned the word over in his mind. There was a divide among people whether or not that word was offensive. Some preferred residual limb and he was fine with that, but he figured he'd earned the right to call it what he wanted.

Taking care of his skin was something he'd learned he needed to be vigilant about to prevent complications. He followed the care instructions but, like little Phoebe, he wasn't always enamored with all the *ru-ules*.

He secured the prosthetic and made his way to the bathroom. He needed to get cleaned up and go in search of food and coffee.

At least he'd had the forethought to ask the desk clerk who'd checked him in yesterday about breakfast. Facing himself in the mirror as he shaved, he questioned his lack of resolve. He hadn't even told Rory and Walt that he'd been Sarge's military handler. He had a feeling Walt suspected the truth, but the man, for whatever reason, hadn't yet confronted him about it. Was the older man trying to protect his granddaughter? Not that Mitch could blame him. Phoebe was the reason he hadn't attempted to claim the dog. Evidently ripping out a sweet little girl's heart was beyond him.

It had absolutely nothing to do with Phoebe's mother. Or her mother's mesmerizing eyes.

Ouch! Blood oozed from a careless swipe of the razor. Cursing his sloppiness, he used a wet washcloth to remove the remaining bits of shaving cream, rinsed, and buried his face in the towel. After he was done, he started to toss the towel onto the floor, but force of habit and too many years in the military prompted him to hang it neatly instead.

He dressed in clean fatigues. Practically a repeat of yesterday's clothing. Fourteen years in the army meant ingrained habits were hard to break. Not wearing them could also mean he was starting a new chapter in his life, something else he needed to get used to. And Cynthie wasn't here to complain if he wore the same things day in and day out. Would Rory complain if he liked wearing his fatigues? Whoa. Where did that thought come from? He'd only just met the woman. After Cynthie broke off their engagement, he'd sworn he would be going through the rest of his life being a selfish bastard—not caring about anyone else, just putting himself first. After all, if *she* couldn't deal with his new reality, how would anyone else be able to?

And how's that solo thing working out for you so far?

He silenced the scoffing voice in his head. Technically he didn't own Sarge. Yes, he'd been the dog's military handler for nearly six years, but that didn't afford him ownership. The army had been Sarge's true owner. Hell, as per tradition, the dog merited a higher rank than his human partner. Mitch knew the military did so to prevent mistreatment of the animals. He couldn't imagine anyone mistreating their dog, no matter the rank.

But if he hadn't sunk into that inviting darkness after losing his leg, he might have realized that Sarge had survived, and he could've fought for him. They could have healed together. No matter what, he'd always regret taking someone else's word regarding the dog's demise. Shame on him.

He pulled on his boot and laced it up, having left the other one attached to the prosthetic for convenience. Slipping his wallet into his back pocket, he grabbed his car keys from the table by the window. Brooding over what couldn't be changed would get him nowhere. Making sure the door locked behind him, not that he had anything in there worth stealing. He went to his vehicle and left his surly mood along with his pitiful belongings back in the room.

Mitch had more time to admire the small town of Loon Lake this morning as he drove through. Yesterday, he had been too focused on finding Sarge to appreciate the quaint beauty of Main Street with its tidy brick-fronted businesses that sported bright-hued awnings, American flags and wooden buckets overflowing with colorful flowers. There was also a town green with a gazebo. It looked like the kind of place that would be crowded on the Fourth of July. Did they have band concerts in the gazebo with people spread out on blankets in the grass? He could easily picture Rory and Phoebe lazing on a blanket listening to the band, watching fireworks.

Could he be happy in a place like this? Could he picture himself in Loon Lake with someone like Rory and her daughter? *Whoa*. Where did that come from? He was not—absolutely *not*—looking to stay permanently in Loon Lake. Or was he? He thought about Rory's big sparkling eyes and—No. He'd opened himself to Cynthie and look what that had gotten him. Nope. He was better off alone. Or doing casual, not staying in one place—or with one person—longer than a mission dictated. That was what he was good at; that was what he knew. And Rory had *permanence* stamped all over her.

Sighing at the direction of his thoughts, he pulled his Toyota into a diagonal parking spot along the main street across from the green. Quite a few of the other spots were taken up by bucket trucks, the kind electric linemen used. Was there a project or something going on in the town?

Dismissing that thought as irrelevant to his current endeavor, he found the place he was looking for. The name of the place, Aunt Polly's, was stenciled in large white letters across two of the four front windows. Above each window were bright red awnings flapping in the morning breeze. He took the rubber band from the cup holder and pulled it over his hand to let it rest on his wrist.

Getting out of the SUV, he fed change into the parking meter and glanced around. He frowned at the large flowerpot next to a bench under the awning. A perfect hiding spot for an enemy, he thought and shook his head. He was still learning to let down his guard back home, in civilian territory. Would he ever fully relax again?

Entering the restaurant, he was hit with scents of coffee, cinnamon and bacon, and his stomach rumbled in response. The place was not only filled with wonderful smells but the buzz of conversation and the clatter of dishes and silverware.

An aisle about six feet wide separated the counter from the tables scattered about the large space and the booths by the windows. Did the customers filling the stools and most of the tables belong to all those bucket trucks?

A trim gray-haired waitress, her hands full carrying a tray loaded with dirty plates, offered a welcoming smile as she passed. "Be back in a jiff."

He nodded and thanked her, feeling people's gazes on him as he waited. Was it his imagination or had the buzz of conversation quieted? That was to be expected since this was a small town. No one seemed unfriendly, just curious as they sized him up. A stranger in town.

Even at this early hour the place was doing a good business. And if the aromas were anything to go by, he could understand why.

The waitress reappeared, her hands empty except for a menu. The pin on her pink uniform said Trudi. "Is a booth by the window, okay? One just opened up. I'll get it wiped down for you if you can hang on for just a sec."

Just on the other side of that flowerpot, he thought but nodded. "Sure. I would have grabbed a stool at the counter, but it's full. You do a big breakfast business."

"More so than usual since we've still got a couple power crews on loan from across the border."

"The border?"

"Canada," she said over her shoulder. "Electric company has reciprocal agreements. Our linemen go there when they need it and vice versa. I was gonna ask if you were with them, but I guess you've already answered my question."

"Nope. Not a lineman." He imagined he had a way to go before he would feel confident in his prosthetic to climb a power pole. Huh, during his time as a Ranger, he hadn't questioned his abilities before plunging into new experiences.

"I don't know how long you've been here in town, but we had some powerful spring storms last weekend. The high winds took down power lines here and in several nearby towns." She lifted a spray bottle from a counter along with a cloth and led him to a booth by a window overlooking the main street, then vigorously wiped down the red tabletop. "Believe it not, last year we had a drought that started a couple of wildfires. But that's New England for you. If you don't like the weather just wait a minute and it'll change."

He simply nodded as she rambled on, not sure if any input was required from him. If anything, he felt comfortable not saying anything about himself, just soaking in her kind demeanor.

"I don't believe I've seen you in here before," she said as she handed him a dog-eared menu.

Mitch took the menu and returned her friendly smile. "I'm new in town."

"Passing through or planning on staying?"

"I'll be staying for a bit." At least long enough to figure out what to do about Sarge. He hadn't totally given up the idea of taking the dog home with him, but at the moment he couldn't. Huh, at the moment, he wasn't even sure where home was going to be.

Trudi nodded. "Then I hope we'll see you in here on a regular basis. Coffee?"

"Yes, please," he said, referring to the coffee. He was still getting used to not being in the army, not being a part of something larger than himself. It felt weird to start thinking of himself as being part of a community. Of course that would only happen if he decided to stay.

"I'll be right back with the coffee while you take

a gander at the menu. Most folks pretty much know the menu by heart. But if you're having trouble deciding, our buckwheat pancakes are popular as are our stuffed French toast options."

She came back with a mug and poured steaming coffee into it. "Find anything that interests you?"

Although the pancakes and French toast were tempting, he decided on the more mundane eggs, hash browns, bacon and toast. Unsure of exactly what the day might bring, he figured his body could use the protein more than the carbs.

The waitress smiled. "Also a good choice. Nice and filling."

Mitch added cream and sugar to his coffee and looked up as a uniformed deputy approached his booth. He noticed the tag pinned above his left breast pocket said Cooper. Not that the name told him anything, since he didn't know anyone in Loon Lake anyway. Well, not *many* people.

"Mind if I sit?" the officer pointed to the empty spot across from Mitch. This not-knowing-anyone thing wasn't going to last long, he reasoned, if people kept coming over to say hello. Not that he minded all that much—in fact, less so than he'd expected.

Mitch nodded. He suspected this was more than a friendly chat. He tapped the spoon over the top of the mug before setting it on the table next to his napkin. This mostly allowed him to buy time to gather his thoughts. The deputy appeared to have a purpose. "Be my guest."

The deputy slid into the booth and rested his forearms on the red Formica tabletop. "First off, I should introduce myself. I'm Riley Cooper."

"Mitch Sawicki." He shifted in his seat as the other man visibly assessed him. "Is this an official visit?"

Cooper shook his head. "Nah. I heard someone new in town was going to be helping Rory out at the farm. Since you're the only one in here not belonging to a power crew that I don't recognize, I took a wild stab that person might be you."

"News travels fast." He'd barely decided to help out on the farm himself and here people in town already knew about it.

"You have no idea. Loon Lake General Store is like information central around here." Cooper grinned, making Mitch crack a slight smile himself.

Mitch recalled passing a wooden barn-red building with an open porch out front and hand-painted signs advertising Vermont cheese and maple syrup. Two ancient gas pumps in the front completed the picture. The place fit perfectly into his image of the town. "Is that the place that looks as if it belongs in another era?"

"That's it. Although much of the town looks like that too, but you'll get used to it."

Not if I don't stay.

The deputy took his silence as agreement because he continued, "Anyway, Tavie Whatley is the owner and if Tavie doesn't know something, it just means it hasn't happened yet."

Mitch laughed. "I'll keep that in mind."

"I don't want to give the wrong impression. She's a bit, well, okay, a *lot*," he chuckled, "of a busybody but kindhearted. We like to call her Loon Lake's benevolent dictator. But you didn't hear that from me."

"Gotcha. Mum's the word." Mitch knew word spread fast in rural areas but found it hard to believe he'd been the subject of gossip already. He'd gone straight to the farm when he drove into town. Aside from a fast-food drive-through last night, this was the first time he'd ventured from the motel. But Loon Lake was a unique kind of place, he guessed.

"So, I heard you were out at the Griffin place talking to Rory." Cooper leaned across the table. "And planning on going back to help Rory with her outbuildings."

"And you came to warn me off?" Why did the fact Rory could be involved with someone disappoint him?

And what business was it of his if she was?

Chapter Five

"Not at all." The deputy held up his left hand, the one with a wedding band. "I'm taken and quite happy about it too. Although I suspect my son James, who's four, has a crush on sweet little Phoebe."

"Your son has good taste," Mitch said. This didn't mean Rory wasn't involved with someone else in town. Guys around here had to have noticed how striking those dark eyes were. And how friendly her demeanor was, and how she visibly adored her daughter... *Get a hold of yourself, Sawicki*, he ordered silently.

"Yeah, Phoebe is cute."

Like her mother, Mitch thought but managed to keep that to himself. He still wasn't quite sure what Cooper's purpose was in stopping by for this *friendly* chat. "A snappy dresser too."

"The princess outfits?" Riley laughed. "Well, my oldest is sadly past that stage and the two younger ones are boys. Still hoping for another girl but gotta convince Meg—that's the missus—that we should try one more time."

"I guess word does travel fast if you already know what I'm supposed to be doing out at the farm." Not only was Mitch curious about how the deputy already knew his business, but he also wanted to get the conversation back on track. Admittedly, though, he was starting to figure out the likely answer to the first question. The rumor mill in Loon Lake never stopped working, apparently.

"Yeah, that." The deputy paused when Trudi brought over Mitch's order.

"Do you need a refill on that coffee yet?" the waitress asked as she set the plate loaded with food in front of him.

Mitch glanced at his half-full mug. "I'm good. Thanks."

"Can I get you anything, Deputy Cooper?" she queried and wiped her hands on her apron.

"Nah. I had to fill in last night so I'm on my way home to Meg and the kids."

"How about a bag of cinnamon crunch scones? Meg will love you forever."

"After she gets through fussing at me for tempting her while she's talking about losing weight.

Don't know where she got that idea from. I think she looks perfect," Cooper responded.

"Good answer." Trudi laughed. "So that's a yes?"

Mitch grinned at the exchange. Small-town life. Was that envy he was feeling? Is this what he wanted for his future? He'd been in Loon Lake such a short time but, even if he left today, he would be taking something away with him.

"Better her fussing than finding out I stopped, and you had those scones and I didn't bring any," the deputy was saying.

"I'll have a bag waiting for you at the counter," the waitress said and trotted off.

Mitch dipped a toast point into the runny egg yolks, which made his mouth water. "So, if you're not warning me off…"

"Just wanted to get a look at you. Rory and Phoebe aren't alone out there anymore, at least not since Walt joined them. But they're good people and I wouldn't want anyone trying to take advantage."

Mitch chewed and swallowed, taking his time deciding how he felt about the deputy's words. His gratitude at knowing locals looked out for the mother and daughter outweighed any annoyance he might harbor for anyone thinking he could be the type of person to take advantage of a woman with a child that depended on her. But he was sure that Cooper meant well, at least as a friend of the Walshes. He wondered what it would be like to have people looking out for him like that—people that weren't his brothers and sisters in arms, anyway. "She's hired me to work on some projects."

The deputy nodded. "How did you hear about the work? Loon Lake is a bit off the beaten path even here in Vermont."

"Actually, I came looking for Bowie Griffin." That was the truth, even if he didn't mention Sarge.

"You serve with him?"

Mitch chuckled. "Do I give off a vibe?"

The deputy grinned. "You do, but Walt may have mentioned it."

"Not directly, no." Still the truth…technically. Mitch wasn't a fan of white lies, but he still was treading carefully in this new environment. He was no longer in a combat zone, but he somehow felt the need to act as if he were once again.

The deputy dipped his head. "But it can be a small world. Not unlike here."

"You were over there?" Mitch asked, hoping to redirect the conversation a bit.

He nodded. "Marines. You?"

"Army. 75th Regiment."

The deputy raised his eyebrows. "Ranger?" Mitch indicated his assent and Cooper continued, "You out for good?"

"I had planned to put in my twenty, but life sometimes has other plans," Mitch said.

Riley Cooper laughed. "Same here. Hope your plans turn out as good as mine have. I may have enjoyed my time while I was in, but I don't regret the life I have now."

Mitch nodded but didn't comment. He wasn't about to admit to a stranger how his plans for marriage and family had been lost along with the lower half of his leg.

Cooper rubbed his chin. "You never did say how you knew about the job."

"And you never said how you knew I had taken the job."

"Fair point. I ran into Walt in the parking lot of the Pic-n-Save—another Loon Lake hot spot—and he mentioned it."

"Wanting to make sure I'm legit?" Mitch didn't blame Walt for looking out for the woman he apparently considered a daughter.

"And to complain that Rory doesn't seem to think he can keep up with things on the farm where they all live."

Mitch finished his breakfast and pushed the plate aside. "If you want references, I can provide them."

Cooper smirked. "That won't be a problem."

"Checked me out already?" Mitch wasn't sure how he felt about being investigated.

Cooper shrugged. "We take care of our own. I still have some contacts in the military."

"And I'm an outsider." Mitch balled up his used napkin and tossed it on the empty plate. It had been a while since he'd felt like that. Even moving around in the military, shared experiences had bonded him with others. He missed that comradery more than he realized. Could he find that here in Loon Lake? Did he want to try?

"You might be a flatlander, but if you help Rory and Walt out, you'll be one of us. I'd better take off. I have a wife and kids waiting at home." Cooper rose and stuck out his hand. "Good to meet you, Sawicki."

Trudi came back with a coffee pot as they were shaking.

"This one's on me, Trudi," Deputy Cooper said and patted her shoulder.

She tutted her tongue. "You know we don't charge our service men for their first meal here."

"But I'm no longer in the army," Mitch protested.

"Don't matter," the waitress replied, shaking her head. "This one's on us."

Riley Cooper chuckled. "For a state full of pacifists, they sure appreciate those who've served. See you around, Sawicki."

"Don't forget your scones," Trudi called, and Cooper quickly changed course and headed for the counter instead of the exit. "Meg would never forgive you."

Mitch listened to the byplay as he pulled out a fresh napkin from the container on the table and wiped his mouth. The waitress held up the pot and he nodded.

"Friendly town," he said as she poured the steaming brew into his mug. The connectedness of these people reminded him of his time in one of those far-flung outposts in Afghanistan. The men had lived practically on top of each other, so privacy was at a premium. "Yeah, everyone looks out for one another. Of course, it's a trade-off because they also know all your business too."

True, but at least here no one in Loon Lake was shooting at him. Just as he had in that outpost, he could learn to accept the good with the bad.

After finishing his second cup of coffee and trying to pay and losing that argument, Mitch settled for leaving a generous tip. As he left, several people nodded as he passed, and he nodded back.

Definitely a friendly little place, he thought as he walked out. The sun hadn't risen very high in the cloudless sky, but it already felt warm on his back as he walked back to his SUV. Yes, this was a pleasant-looking town. Even before his broken engagement, he'd never given much thought to life after the army. Being an Army Ranger had been his dream for so long that once he achieved his dream, he hadn't thought beyond that. In hindsight he realized that attitude had been a mistake on his part. Now that he thought about it, he had trouble imagining his ex-fiancée following him from post to post. He imagined someone like Rory would follow her husband.

He shook his head as he used the key fob to unlock his Toyota. What had gotten into him? He barely knew the woman and was already ascribing wifely characteristics to her. He slipped behind the wheel and started the engine.

At the turnoff to the farm, he paused for a moment. Did he really want to go back knowing he wouldn't be bringing Sarge home with him? At least not yet. Maybe not ever. He winced at that last thought.

Hanging around for a while would at least ease his mind about Sarge's future if the dog stayed on the farm. He glanced in the rearview mirror.

"Is that what you're telling yourself?" he asked his reflection as he drove toward the house and an alluring pair of brown eyes.

Phoebe must've seen or heard him coming because she was on the porch jumping up and down when he pulled up to the large two-story dove-gray farmhouse.

"Mr. Mitch. Mr. Mitch."

He took a moment to admire the house with its bright white trim, tall sash windows and dark blue shutters. Yesterday, he'd been so caught up in thoughts of Sarge that he hadn't taken the time to observe his surroundings. A cracked cement sidewalk led to a covered porch and the open front door where Phoebe was waiting.

He noticed despite her obvious eagerness that Phoebe was staying on the porch. He hurried out of the SUV and slammed his door shut. Today the little princess, dressed in blue overalls and a bright red T-shirt, looking every inch the farmer. She came scrambling down the steps and into the driveway. She might have changed out of the princess outfit, but she still wore the red boots and the homemade crown.

Seeing her standing there, he realized Rory wasn't the only one he'd been looking forward to seeing again. After getting dumped his reaction had been to give up on his plans for a wife and family. But that had been a kneejerk one. One broken engagement was hardly reason to make such a sweeping decision about the rest of his life.

"You missed all the 'citement," Phoebe said.

Excitement? It was barely eight in the morning. How much excitement could they have had? He glanced at Phoebe's outfit again. Was she a princess farmer today? Her obsession with fairy tales and the fact she was only four made him surmise that her definition of excitement might not match his.

"Mommy was crying and everything. But she pretended she wasn't. She does that sometimes. Says she wasn't crying when she is."

Kinda like his own mother. Damn. Maybe this *was* serious. "What happened?"

That's when he noticed Walt standing just inside the doorway, sipping from a white ceramic mug. The older man didn't look upset, so the problem couldn't be too catastrophic.

Walt stepped forward. "Something got into her plants last night and trashed them."

"Something?" Mitch tensed and pulled in on himself in a semicrouch. Turning, he scanned the surrounding area looking for telltale signs of enemy encroachment.

"Whatever it was, it's long gone, son."

Walt's voice brought him back to the present. Warmth rose in his face. *Expecting to see enemy combatants in the tree line, Sawicki?*

Nothing like embarrassing himself in front of a marine and a four-year-old. Mitch straightened and turned back to face Walt. He stiffened, momentarily abashed to realize he really hadn't adjusted as well as he'd thought to civilian life.

But instead of ridicule or that dreaded pity, the older man's look held understanding. "It happens."

"What happens, Grandpa G?" Phoebe asked.

"Critters helping themselves to your mother's crops," Walt said.

Mitch knew he hadn't been referring to that. He silently saluted the man and made a mental note to ask him about his service. Mitch was filled with a quiet sense of gratitude, one veteran to another. He didn't even have to voice it; meeting Walt's eyes was sufficient.

"Does she have fencing?" Mitch asked.

Walt nodded. "Looks like it got knocked over in one spot."

"That's why Mommy wouldn't let Sarge go out. Because she was afraid it might be a *big ole bear*," Phoebe said.

Sounded to him as if Phoebe was imitating someone but he wasn't sure who. He shuddered at the thought of Sarge with his three legs tangling with a bear. "Well then, I'm glad you kept him safe in the house." *Even if I couldn't keep Sarge safe back in Afghanistan.*

"Yeah, me too." Phoebe nodded her head vigorously. "I love him so much."

I know you do, Princess. Mitch ignored the

gnawing in the pit of his stomach. "Do you get many bears around here?"

"Lots and lots," Phoebe told him.

Mitch glanced at Walt, who shrugged and said, "Some."

Phoebe ran over and grabbed Mitch's hand to guide him to the porch. The gesture surprised him, but he found he didn't really mind. Truth be told he liked it. His thoughts went back to the bear and he tightened his hold on her hand, ready to fight off any threats to this child.

"Do you like my outfit? It's my coworker clothes."

"Coworker clothes?" he asked.

"Uh-huh," she said and did a little skip. "If I'm going to be your coworker, I need to look like a farmer."

"And you look like the perfect farmer."

"Mommy said I could be a coworker as long as I didn't get in your way. I won't get in your way, will I, Mr. Mitch?"

"I'm sure you'll be fine," he told her.

Walt snorted and shook his head. Mitch couldn't help grinning and shrugging when he met the older man's gaze.

Sarge came bounding out of the open front door, scrambling down the porch steps to reach Mitch. The dog promptly sat down in front of him, panting and doing that canine smile thing that melted Mitch's heart every time. He probably shouldn't admit that since he and Sarge were both battle-hardened ex-soldiers, but it was the truth.

"Well, good morning to you too." Mitch rubbed the dog's ears with his free hand. Phoebe still had a tight grip on the other.

Sarge's tail thumped on the ground as he leaned into Mitch's palm.

"He really likes you, Mr. Mitch."

"Well, the feeling is mutual."

The little girl scowled up at him. "I don't know what *moo-shall* means."

"It means I like him too," he told her, smiling slightly.

"Oh, okay. Thank you for 'splaining things to me. I don't like it when people say stuff I don't understand."

"I noticed that," Mitch told her. Damn, but she had the ability to melt his heart too. *Going soft, Sawicki? Especially for a little girl you barely even know?*

"Here's where everyone's been hiding." Rory appeared in the doorway, wearing an outfit similar to her daughter's, red T-shirt under overalls, but minus the boots and crown.

Her outfit wasn't some fashion statement but practical working clothes…and yet he found them as appealing as a sexy cocktail dress.

"Funny how when it's time to clean up, everyone disappears. Even the dog," she said.

Sarge yipped as if putting up a defense at her accusation and her face split into a soft smile.

Mitch swallowed hard and his heart rate kicked up at the sight of that broad grin. It may have been directed at Sarge, but he was the one reacting to it. He had to fight the urge to flick the rubber band he wore around his wrist. Only this wouldn't be to disrupt the neural pathways in his brain that caused phantom pain but to remind himself that he didn't come here looking to get involved with a woman. Especially one with a child. He needed to remember his plan to live a selfish life. Anyone responsible for a little one didn't have the luxury of caring mostly about their own behavior. So that right there disqualified him.

He blamed his reaction to Rory on the situation. How she'd made him feel earlier had softened him up. Yep, that was it. He shushed the inner critic who scoffed at his reasoning. He came to Loon Lake looking for his dog. Nothing more. He wasn't looking for a relationship. Or a family. His dog was all he wanted...wasn't it?

Chapter Six

He might not have come here looking to get involved with anyone, but the sight of Rory and her fresh face and the way her teeth showed when she smiled kick-started his heart. He might have to re-evaluate his stance on that.

"Did either of you think to offer Mitch some breakfast?" Rory asked, her gaze darting between her uncle and her daughter.

"Uh-oh, Mommy, did we break a rule?" Phoebe squeezed Mitch's hand.

He returned the gentle contact, glanced down at the girl with her big eyes and pulled a face so she giggled. *You can't seem to help yourself around the Walsh women*, he admonished himself lightly.

"Well, then it looks as though I need to do it,"

Rory said. "Mitch, would you like some breakfast? Or some coffee?"

"No thank you. I stopped at the cafe across from the town green for breakfast and coffee." His gaze went to Walt. "Met some of the locals, including a chatty uniformed deputy."

Walt met his eyes head on, challenge lurking in their dark depths. "Can't be too careful these days."

Rory clicked her tongue in evident disapproval and turned to her uncle. "Walt. Don't tell me you sicced Riley on him."

"Okay, I won't," Walt said and shrugged, looking anything but contrite which had Rory sighing and shaking her head.

But Walt's attitude didn't bother Mitch because he understood the concept of looking out for your own. If some guy started hanging around his mother, he'd sure want to know more about him. Of course, taking off the way he had meant he didn't know who might be hanging around his mother. He made a mental note to call and check on her again. He'd avoided it until now because he wasn't sure he wanted to explain what he was doing in Loon Lake. But he owed it to her to ask her how she was doing and to let her know what he was up to—and besides, he *did* genuinely care. Even if he couldn't imagine living in the same house with his family as Rory did with hers.

Rory rolled her eyes at her uncle before turning her attention back to Mitch. "I hope Riley didn't give you the third degree or anything."

"Nah. It was all very civil, just a mild interrogation. No water boarding or anything like that," he joked but when he saw her obvious distress, he hastened to add, "Don't sweat it. I've had worse as a horny teenager picking up a date and being faced with her father. An encounter with a deputy was hardly a blip on the radar."

"What does *horny* mean, Mr. Mitch?"

Mitch swallowed. Damn. He needed to watch his language around her. He mouthed the word *sorry* to Rory, who was blushing. Even Sarge made a noise in his throat as if scolding him. Mitch lifted an eyebrow at the dog. *Et tu Brute?*

She acknowledged his apology with a lift of her chin. "He must've had some hair sticking out from the side of his head near his ears."

"You mean like the great horned owl?" Phoebe asked, her eyes widening.

Mitch looked between the two of them. What in the heck were they talking about? This wasn't the first time he'd felt he'd tumbled down a rabbit hole since meeting them. "You're comparing me to an owl?"

"Don't you like owls, Mr. Mitch?" asked the little girl, sounding incredulous.

"Owls?" He glanced to Walt for help, but the other man was just grinning from ear to ear and shaking his head. Probably trying to picture Mitch with hair sticking out above his ears. Or laughing at him for sticking his foot in his mouth in the first place. Mitch sighed. Served him right for not policing his language in front of a four-year-old. Although he had to admit that following Phoebe's conversation U-turns were sometimes challenging. But he found he enjoyed her whimsical take on the world.

"Owls are my favoritest thing in the whole world. I'm gonna be an *orange-thologist* when I grow up. Mommy says those are the people who know all about birds. Isn't that right, Mommy?"

"That's right," Rory said, her lips twitching as if she too was thoroughly enjoying Mitch's confusion.

Before he could recover, Phoebe was tugging on his hand. "Did you know owls are birds?"

"I had heard that somewhere, yes," he said and wiped his free hand over his mouth, finally getting into the spirit of this strange conversation, "and I'm sure you'll make a wonderful ornithologist."

She dropped his hand to perform an elaborate dance twirl. "And a princess too, cuz Mommy says I can be anything I want. And I want to be one of those too, huh, Mommy?"

"But I thought you were a princess already." Mitch put his hand over his chest and feigned surprise. "You certainly looked like one yesterday."

"That was just pretend." She giggled. "Mommy made the crown for me from *leminum* foil. Real princess crowns have diamonds. Lots and lots of them, but Mommy said she didn't have any diamonds just lying around."

"No diamonds lying around?" Mitch looked to Rory who gave him a soft smile that made his heart skip a beat. Was that smile because he was playing along? Did he want it to be something more? "That's too bad about the diamonds, but your mommy is very inventive."

Rory might not be wearing any rings right now but he had to wonder if Phoebe's father had ever given her a diamond. His ex had offered to return the ring he'd given her but he had no use for it and told her to keep it.

Phoebe scowled. "I don't know what in-inbentive means."

"It means she's good at making crowns that look real even without diamonds."

"She's good at lots of stuff," Phoebe assured him.

"I'll bet." The one thing Mitch was dying to know was how good she was at kissing, but that wasn't something he could admit out loud, especially in front of others.

In his peripheral vision, Mitch caught Walt attempting to slip away as if seeing his chance and hoping to make an escape. *That's what I'd do*, Mitch thought as he watched him, but didn't give the other man's exit away.

Evidently Rory saw it too because she stopped him with a hand on his arm. "Not so fast. Please tell me Riley just happened to be at Aunt Polly's the same time as Mitch this morning."

Phoebe pulled on Mitch's hand before Walt could respond. "You went to Aunt Polly's?" she asked, heaving a big sigh. "I love going there to get pancakes. They're the yummiest. What kind did you have?"

"I'm sure they are, but I didn't have the pancakes. Maybe next time." He smiled at her openly hopeful expression. Nothing subtle about her. "Of course, I'd have to bring someone with me to show me which ones to order. Do you know someone like that?"

"Me," she shouted, jumping up and down and twirling crookedly.

"*Phee-bee*," her mother drew out her name as if in disbelief she'd been so bold.

Phoebe stopped her gymnastics but confronted her mother. "But, Mommy, he asked me and I does know the best ones."

"Then you'll have to be my pancake adviser," Mitch told her with a wide grin. She really was a cute kid and taking her—and her mom, of course—for pancakes seemed simple enough.

Phoebe gave him a questioning look. "Does being a pancakes visor mean I can come with you?"

"Yes, Princess, it does."

"Yippee. Did you hear that, Mommy?" She leaned toward her mother. "And he called me Princess."

Rory gave her an indulgent smile. "Yes, I think we all heard it."

"Maybe your mom would like to come with us," he suggested before he could police his words.

Oh man, what in the world was he doing? Asking Rory out for pancakes sounded an awful lot like a date. What happened to a simple outing? Did breakfast count as an official date?

Sarge yipped as if answering Mitch's silent questions and he glared at his former partner. *What do you know? You're a dog!* If he didn't know better, he'd swear that dog was smirking at him. Of course that was impossible—he glanced at the others. Or not.

"Well… I, um, do love their pancakes too," Rory said, her cheeks pink and her eyes compelling, magnetic.

"Then it's a date." Once again, the words were out of his mouth before he could stop them. But he felt as though she'd put a spell on him with those twinkling eyes. That was it. They'd all cast some sort of spell over him, making him forget his vow to be selfish.

Well, that was that. He had a date. The first one since his life had taken such a drastic change. That thought make his gut tighten. Rory had no idea what had happened to him. Would she, like his ex, reject him because of it? He didn't want to believe she would, but how could he be sure?

No doubt he needed to tell her. But how? *Oh, by the way, I'm missing the bottom half of my left leg? You know that dog you adopted? Yeah, well, he's not the only one missing a limb. And, as if that weren't enough, I do know Sarge. He was my loyal partner for six years. He's the real reason I came in the first place. I had every intention of taking*

*him back to North Carolina with me without much
regard to how you felt about it.*

Oh man. What had he gotten himself into?

And more importantly, how would he get out of
this without hurting Phoebe and Rory? The thought
of doing anything to harm them was like acid being
poured on his soul. And he'd only known them such
a short amount of time.

He sighed. *I'm in trouble*, he thought to himself,
shooting a glance at Sarge.

Rory gave her meddling uncle a look that promised this thing with Riley questioning Mitch wasn't
over yet. She loved Walt to death and owed him so
much for being there when she needed him, not only
after the death of her parents but after her divorce
when she'd been overwhelmed with working, taking
care of Phoebe and then a dog. If not for Walt doing
what he could, like taking Phoebe and the dog to the
park, she didn't know how she would have coped.

And if Mitch was going to stick around, she
needed to caution him about what he said in front
of Phoebe, aka the sponge. Sponge? More like a
vacuum cleaner, since she picked up absolutely everything.

"Phoebe, could you show Mr. Mitch where the
vegetable patch is? I need to talk to Grandpa G.
We'll catch up. You can take Sarge with you."

The dog woofed and wagged his tail. Rory shook
her head. Sometimes she swore that animal understood everything that they said.

"Okay," Phoebe said and grabbed Mitch's hand.

She waited until they were out of earshot, and she turned on Walt. "What's this about Riley Cooper questioning Mitch?"

"Riley bumped into him at Polly's," Walt said innocently.

"Purely coincidental of course." Rory gave her uncle a look. She normally didn't mind Loon Lake being such a close-knit town, but sometimes it was a bit annoying. She didn't need every man in town looking out for her, thank you very much; in fact, Rory was a capable single mom who could screen her own employees. And Mitch might be a bit rough around the edges, but he certainly didn't merit a military-grade grilling from a family friend.

"And, before you say anything more, I did not ask Riley to ambush him at the cafe." Walt grimaced. "I admit I may have asked Riley to check him out through his military contacts. So what if I did? I was looking out for you and the little one."

"I know and I appreciate it." She gave her uncle a quick hug. Her uncle loved her but she knew he wasn't a physically demonstrative man. Except perhaps with Phoebe, who had him wrapped around her little finger.

Of course he'd also done his absolute best when she and Bowie had lost their parents. She'd always carry the emotional scars of losing them but she had Walt to thank for becoming a well-adjusted adult. Well, mostly well-adjusted she amended with an internal grin.

She sighed, hating that she was going to ask this but asking anyway. "And what did Riley find out?"

"He checks out. Was in the army and distinguished himself as a Ranger. He was a dog handler."

"And you're thinking he may have known Sarge?"

"That dog wouldn't have taken to him as quick as he did if he hadn't."

"So, you're thinking what?"

"That it's pretty coincidental that he shows up here out of the blue. And he happens to have worked with the dog you adopted? Seems like too much of a good thing to me."

"But we've had Sarge for a whole year. Why would he come now? Maybe we should just ask him. I don't like sneaking around." She was taken aback at the idea Mitch could have been lying by omission to her. And Phoebe. Was he here to take their beloved pet from the family? Remembering those green eyes made her feel all warm inside, and she shoved the feeling down deep inside. She wouldn't let anyone come between Phoebe and Sarge.

"No one is sneaking around," Walt insisted.

"You asked Riley to check up on him."

"And I explained that."

She sighed. "Do you honestly think we should ask him about Sarge?"

Walt shrugged. "Let's wait and see if the boy has an explanation. Riley says he likes him and he's got a good sense about people."

"Fine," she muttered and started toward the ruined vegetable patch.

Then it's a date.

Mitch's words tumbled around in her head like loose change in a dryer. Did he mean for his invitation to be a date or was that just an expression? Lots of people used that phrasing and didn't mean anything remotely romantic by it.

And besides, he'd invited Phoebe first. After she had practically begged him to. So, this couldn't be a date. He was just responding to a child's not-so-subtle request. She should be relieved. And she was. Yep, she sure was.

So why are you already planning what to wear for this non-date? She tried to shush the annoying voice…and failed miserably.

Chapter Seven

"Rory?"

"Huh?" She'd been so involved in her thoughts she'd retreated into herself. Heat blooming in her cheeks, she turned to find Mitch, Walt and Phoebe staring at her. Even Sarge was looking at her with an expectant expression. They'd reached the ruined vegetable patch with its destroyed fencing.

"I was wondering if you wanted the fence rebuilt or to put something else in place," Mitch said, giving her a look that suggested he'd asked more than once, increasing the heat making its way to her face.

She sighed as she surveyed the damage done the previous night by a hungry bear. "There's not a lot left to salvage."

"Is this why you want a greenhouse?" Mitch asked.

"Not sure that would help if a bear came along. Although it would slow it down a bit, but it's my understanding that bears spend much of their time looking for and figuring out how to get food. I'm not sure what I can do to deter it. Especially if it thinks it can come here for an easy meal."

She'd fenced the area to keep out rabbits and deer but obviously a fence was not the same as bear proofing the property. She'd lost her carrots and beets before they'd even had a chance to mature. The bear had pretty much trashed everything else in order to get to her roots and tubers, resulting in hundreds if not thousands of dollars of lost inventory.

"What could we do to discourage it? Make it not so easy," Mitch asked.

Phoebe, who was still bouncing around, reached for Mitch's hand again. "Grandpa G said he could shoot it, but Mommy said you can't kill a bear for being a bear."

"I gotta agree with your mom on that one." Mitch turned to Walt. "Do you have any other ideas?"

Walt scratched his scalp. "We can do a few things to discourage it. Its determination will depend on how hungry it is."

Rory listened as Mitch and Walt discussed options. The fact Mitch had turned to Walt for advice warmed her heart. She didn't want Mitch's presence to make it seem as if he was going to replace Walt in any way. Walt had been a bit touchy after his heart attack and retiring from his second career as a sheriff's deputy. Well, okay, more than a bit, but she knew she hadn't helped the matter with her knee-jerk reaction of smothering.

But losing your parents at age twelve stole your innocence, taught you how random and cruel life could be. Even today, with the benefit of hindsight, she held tight to those she loved. She hated that Bowie risked his life by being in Special Forces. She would never admit it to Walt, but she breathed a sigh of relief when he retired from the sheriff's department.

As for Phoebe, she had to force herself to let her daughter spend time away from her. If not for knowing Phoebe needed to spend time with her dad, she'd refuse to let her go. As it was, her stomach ached until she had her safely back home despite the fact Curt was a good dad, careful and caring.

"Rory?"

Once again, Mitch's voice broke into her thoughts. "Pardon?"

"What about your chickens?"

"I don't have any yet."

"I meant, what are your plans for protecting them? I looked up how to keep them safe."

She laughed. "And you found out the world is full of predators whose sole purpose is to kill chickens? Besides foxes, I mean."

"Pretty much, yeah."

He grinned, sending her heart rate soaring. Their conversation might be concerning mundane matters, but her reaction to him was anything but mundane. She needed to get a handle on this. How could a simple gesture with one's lips mean so much? She hadn't even been this physically aware and fascinated by Curt.

"But, Mommy, why would somebody want to kill our chickens? That's not very nice," Phoebe asked, looking concerned.

"Don't worry, sweetie, we'll do everything we can to keep our chickens safe. That's why we're going to build a henhouse and fence in an area to keep them safe."

"But you put up a fence for your veg-a-tables and the bear still got them."

"I'll be sure it's bear proof," Mitch assured her.

And owl proof, she added silently. But thank goodness they only hunted at night. She glanced at the sky. Hawks could be a problem, but no need to distress Phoebe at this point. "I'm sure Elliott's mom will be able to give us all sorts of advice,"

"Do you know Elliott, Mr. Mitch?"

"No, I'm afraid I don't."

"He's my friend but he's only three so he's still a little kid," she told him.

"I see." Mitch nodded, his lips twitching.

Rory watched Mitch get his need to laugh under control. As caring as Curt was towards Phoebe, he wasn't always as aware of her feelings as Mitch seemed to be. Curt always apologized for hurting her feelings but by then the damage was done. Plus, she didn't want any of Phoebe's enthusiasm to be dampened. At least not yet. As she got older she would experience enough disappointment. Why start now?

Who knew respecting her daughter's feelings could be so appealing? But jeez, what he must think of the lot of them? From Walt setting Deputy Cooper on him to Phoebe wrangling a breakfast invitation. She wouldn't be surprised if he wanted to wash his hands of them.

"I did some research and got most of that covered, including the henhouse," he was saying, sounding confident he had this under control.

And why shouldn't he she asked herself. He was Special Forces, and she knew from her brother what it took to simply get through training. So what was Mitch Sawicki doing on her farm? Oh, she wasn't complaining. She studied him from under her lashes. Nope. Not one bit.

"You work fast," she said, hoping her voice sounded normal despite her racing heart.

"Yeah, I've got it covered."

"You gonna build Mommy a house for the chickens?" Phoebe asked.

"That's the plan."

"So quickly? But how?" Rory asked. She hadn't been kidding when she said keeping fowl safe from predators wasn't easy. And yet, he seemed self-assured, and she found she liked that confidence. She liked it a lot.

"Well, I've got a prefab shed coming."

"A shed?" He wanted to put her chickens in a shed? And what would that cost? "I—"

"And don't worry about cost. I know a guy and got a good deal," Walt said.

Was her uncle a mind reader? "I can't let you pay for it."

Walt shrugged. "I can't take it with me."

"Considering you're not going anywhere, you might need it," she said. She hated when he talked like that. Of course she knew he wasn't immortal but she didn't want it thrown in her face.

"It's a done deal," Walt said with finality.

"And it's a starting point. Better than starting from scratch. I figure Walt and I can make modifications to it to turn it into a state-of-the-art henhouse. Using the shed as a starting point will help the process along." Mitch turned to her uncle. "If you're willing, Walt."

"I'm sure between the two of us we can figure something out," Walt said.

"So, I get my chickens?" Excitement won out over her financial concerns. If the business took off, she'd be able to repay Walt. Not only did she want to be able to offer her customers fresh eggs, but she'd also be able to use them to make some baked goods to showcase her farm-to-table offerings. She had to caution herself not to twirl and dance like Phoebe.

"Looks like it." Walt nodded. "By the way, Mitch, where have you been staying?"

Mitch gave him a quizzical look. "The Stargazer Inn, on the edge of town."

Walt shook his head. "I don't think we're paying

you enough for that. Besides, we have a perfectly sound bunkhouse sitting empty."

What was Walt doing? He'd done an about-face. Or had whatever he'd found out about the newcomer satisfied him?

Mitch shrugged. "Like I said, I didn't come looking for a handout."

Walt harrumphed. "This won't be a handout. Call it a perk of this pretty lousy employment opportunity," Walt said and looked to her with an unspoken question in his eyes.

"Now who's doing a lousy job of selling this opportunity?" she joked, meeting Walt's gaze she gave a slight nod to indicate she was on board with this despite some misgivings. Did she want him here all the time? Yes, she did, but that was the problem. She'd have temptation practically on her doorstep.

"What's everyone talking about?" Phoebe asked, her head swiveling between the adults.

"We're talking about Mr. Mitch staying here on the farm," she told her daughter.

Phoebe clapped her hands. "Goody! Mr. Mitch is gonna live with us now."

Rory rolled her eyes. Now who was opening their big mouth in front of Phoebe? She should have phrased that better. She could just imagine Phoebe telling people Mitch had come to live with them. Gossip and speculation would be flying around town. "Not exactly living with us, but he'll be staying in the little bunkhouse behind the barn. There's a difference, sweetie. Do you understand?"

"No," Phoebe said as if that ended it and turned her attention to Mitch. "Will you be able to read me a bedtime story?"

"Sweetie, I just said he's not going to be living in the house with us," Rory reiterated. Damn, she should have known better than to mention any of this in front of her daughter. Besides, Mitch hadn't even agreed to come and stay yet.

Phoebe stuck her lower lip out. "But you said—"

"If I stay, it will be in the bunkhouse, but maybe at some point I can find the time to read a story to my coworker," Mitch told Phoebe. "Maybe at lunchtime or something. We can call them lunchtime stories."

Mitch's gaze met Rory's and she nodded. Looked as though he understood the implications inherent in Phoebe telling others Mitch was reading her bedtime stories. This might be the twenty-first century, but Loon Lake was still a small town where gossip reigned. Of course, there was always the possibility he didn't want to be associated with her in a romantic context. The thought brought her crashing to earth with a thud. She might be thinking about how his lips would feel but that didn't mean he was having any thoughts like that whatsoever about her.

"Can you read from my owl book?" Phoebe asked, her tone hopeful.

"Sure, if it's okay with your mom," Mitch said.

"Mommy?"

"I'm sure that can be arranged." Rory smiled and threw him a look that said he may regret agreeing.

Phoebe's "owl book" was a five-hundred-page tome containing everything anyone ever wanted to know about owls. Nothing childish about it, but Phoebe had been in love with it from the moment she set eyes on it in the bookstore. Rory had to admit it was a beautiful volume full of slick, colorful pictures.

Sarge woofed as if he too liked the arrangement. Rory didn't miss the look of mutual adoration that passed between the dog and Mitch. She suspected there was some sort of history there but decided to let Mitch explain it when he was ready.

She should have been more upset at the prospect of a lie by omission. So, why wasn't she? Was she letting her attraction to Mitch cloud her judgment? But on the other hand, Walt seemed to like and trust Mitch so that was good with her.

"So, it's settled?" Walt asked and when Rory nodded, he continued, "If you'll help me clean out the unused bunkhouse, I'm sure Rory could make it very comfortable. That girl has a knack for turning places into something more than a simple shelter. She helped Bowie with this place. Used her magic touch to transform it from a neglected relic to a real home. Oh, wait, Bowie and I *were* the neglected relics."

"Walt," she said and *tsked* her tongue.

Walt grinned. "She did pretty good with the house too."

"What's a relic?" Phoebe asked, scrunching up her nose.

"Someone who is really, really old," Rory told her, grinning at Walt, who just laughed.

Later that morning after they'd worked in the ruined garden and returned it to some semblance of order, she turned her attention to Mitch. "Would you like to join us for lunch?"

Oh man, why had she asked that? Living in the bunkhouse and joining them for meals sounded an awful lot like getting involved. Did she want that?

One thing she'd promised herself after the divorce was that she wouldn't allow a parade of men into Phoebe's life. Not that she ever had a parade of men in her life and she hadn't even casually dated after her marriage ended.

But then she'd never felt so tempted by anyone as she did with Mitch.

Mitch debated the question, giving the simple invitation more importance than it deserved. What was wrong with him? He'd just agreed to living on the premises and yet now he was dithering over an invitation to lunch. It was just the meal between breakfast and dinner...but it meant spending personal time with Rory. And the more time he spent with her and Phoebe, the tighter the noose would be around his neck. He could justify moving into the bunkhouse as a business decision but sharing meals changed the dynamic. At least that's what he was telling himself.

Adjusting to civilian life wasn't easy but Walt seemed to understand his difficulties and they communicated without having to spell things out. And helping Rory bring her farm-to-table dream to fruition gave him something to work toward.

He'd come to Loon Lake to get his dog back. Period. He hadn't come to fall for a single mother and her daughter, no matter how attractive the woman or precocious the daughter. He had to get his own life sorted out… How could he take responsibility for two others?

Was he staying here to help or just delaying the inevitable? Leaving here without Sarge felt too much like defeat but he wasn't going to break a little girl's heart to get what he wanted.

"Mr. Mitch?" A tiny hand tugged on his pant leg and he glanced down. "I think you should say yes. My mommy's maca-mony and cheese is the yummiest, even if it's not from a box."

Rory chuckled. "Yeah, pair it with a fine Two Buck Chuck chardonnay and you have a gourmet meal."

His gaze met hers and his heart lurched. Her smile softened her features and he had to remind himself he wasn't in a place in his life where he could get involved. And he was sure Rory, as a single mother, wasn't looking for casual sex. And that was all he could offer.

He realized with a jolt that he had two ladies looking at him. He cleared his throat, feeling warmth rise in his cheeks. He'd tell them no, thank you. Simple. "Thank you, I…uh, sure. I hate to miss the yummiest mac and cheese."

What? No, no, *no*. That refusal sounded an awful lot like a yes. Maybe he could just this once, but as soon as the bunkhouse was fixed up, he would buy a small fridge and take his meals there. Then who could say he was making a moved on the very fine Ms. Rory Walsh?

Phoebe clapped her hands. "You won't be sorry, Mr. Mitch."

He was already sorry, but he smiled and nodded. He couldn't disappoint Phoebe. Of course he'd have to be careful going forward. Not disappointing the precious little girl could lead to trouble if he wasn't careful.

When he'd gotten engaged, he'd imagined having a family of his own in the future. It had been a someday plan but Rory and Phoebe were a ready-made family. Was he ready for something like that?

Rory had been convinced for a moment that he was going to refuse. She would have bet on it, in fact. She smiled to herself because she was pretty sure by his reaction that he'd surprised himself with his acceptance. Yeah, her precocious daughter had that effect. Rory wasn't sure if that was good or bad when it came to Mitch.

"Is there anything I can do to help?" he asked once he'd joined them in the kitchen at the farmhouse after putting away the garden tools.

"Would you mind slicing some cucumbers and tomatoes for the salad?" She motioned toward the items she'd laid out on the counter. She'd come in earlier than the others to get lunch started.

He leaned toward Phoebe. "You didn't tell me this was going to involve eating salad too," he said in a stage whisper.

Phoebe giggled. "Mommy says that sometimes you gotta eat stuff that's good for you too."

Rory enjoyed listening to the by-play between them.

"Eating healthy is a thing with her," Walt said as he stepped into the kitchen.

Sarge was right behind him and made a beeline for Mitch, his toenails clicking on the worn vinyl flooring.

"Hey, I'm letting you have mac and cheese," Rory told her uncle as she watched the interaction between Mitch and the dog.

"Yeah, but you're gonna make me eat salad too," Walt grumbled, but his tone was good-natured as he went to the sink to wash his hands.

"Do you like salad, Mr. Mitch?"

"Yes, I do."

"If you came to live with us, you could eat salad all the time," Phoebe told as if that was a big selling point.

"That's a very tempting offer, Princess," he said and continued to rub the dog's ears and stroke the top of his head.

"I'm going to go get my owl book to show Mr. Mitch," Phoebe said and dashed from the room.

Sarge watched Phoebe leave, gave Mitch a 'sorry' look and rushed to catch up with her.

"Well, now I know where I stand," Mitch said, huffing out a low throaty laugh.

His laugh washed over her.

Just as Walt had done, Mitch washed his hands in the kitchen sink while she pulled the casserole dish from the oven, filling the room with the aroma of warm cheese.

After drying his hands with the towel Walt handed him, Mitch began slicing the cucumbers and tomatoes, tossing them into the salad as he did so. She enjoyed having Mitch in the kitchen, acting all domestic.

"When you see this book you may regret agreeing to read it," she warned Mitch with a smile.

His gaze captured hers for a moment and she felt a thrill skitter up her spine.

"So, not a little picture book?" Mitch asked and frowned when Walt snorted.

"Oh, it has pictures," she said with a grin.

Before Mitch could react to either one of them, Phoebe came back into the kitchen, lugging a large book. It was heavy and she grunted as she hefted it onto the table. He bent over it on the table and began flipping through it.

"Wanna smell it? It's okay if you do."

"Smell it?" He looked to Rory as if asking her if he'd heard that right.

Once again, Rory offered him a smile. She really shouldn't be enjoying his confusion but she was. Not only was she proud of her daughter for taking such an interest in something and wanting to find out all she could but she trusted Mitch to respect that.

Maybe she was misplacing that trust since she still suspected he hadn't been completely truthful about any previous relationship with Sarge. Was she making a mistake?

"Smell it?" he repeated.

"Uh-huh. I like to do that with books. Uncle Bo says it's weird, but Mommy says that's cuz Uncle Bo doesn't love books as much as me. Do you like books, Mr. Mitch?"

"I like books, although I suspect not as much as you since I've never considered smelling one,"he said.

"Let's set the book aside for now, sweetie," Rory brought the casserole to the table and set it on the hot pad she'd already put on the table.

During the meal she couldn't help sneaking glances at Mitch as he listened to Phoebe telling him all she knew about owls.

Her stomach unleashed a swarm of butterflies at the thought of how seamlessly Mitch integrated into their little family.

It's just lunch, she scolded herself but whenever her gaze caught his, he smiled at her. She groaned inwardly because some people might say that was the sort of smile women had been building futures around for ages.

Chapter Eight

Mitch surveyed the newly cleaned and hastily furnished bunkhouse later that night. The place was cozy and comfortable, but it resembled a hotel room, lacking permanence. The thought of a permanent residence gave Mitch a pang in his chest. The last time he'd had one of those was when he was a kid and lived with his mom in the small bungalow she'd scrimped and saved to afford.

His mother might have raised him alone but she'd always managed to provide a stable environment for them. He might not have always had the most expensive toys or gadgets but his mother always made sure he'd had enough not to feel deprived. The middle-class neighborhood they'd lived in was safe and well-kept.

Once he'd joined the army, he'd lived in bachelor

quarters or in camps while on deployment. After he and Cynthie had gotten together, he'd stay part of the time at her place. But that's what it had been… her place.

"Is there a problem?"

Rory's question broke into his musings. He turned to her and the gathering disappointment in her expression tightened his gut. He hated to appear ungrateful.

"I'm a little overwhelmed," he admitted. Normally, he wouldn't admit such a weakness, but he felt responsible for that uncertainty in her face. And he didn't like it. "You and Walt have both gone to a lot of trouble for me. A virtual stranger."

"Well, you said you know Bowie so not a complete stranger."

He winced inwardly at her assertion. *Come clean and do it now*, an inner voice pleaded—or was that his conscience?

As if sensing his inner conflict, Sarge whined and came to stand next to him and lean against Mitch's leg.

Mitch vigorously rubbed the dog's ears and cupped his head between his hands. "Aren't you a good boy."

Sarge's entire body squirmed as Mitch continued to massage him and speak to him using a higher-than-normal octave to praise him, something they'd taught him when he'd worked as a dog handler.

"Are you sure you two don't know one another?"

Rory asked. "I don't think he's ever reacted like that to someone he's just met."

"Dogs have always liked me," Mitch said.

He debated telling the truth. Getting Sarge back had been his whole purpose in coming. So why was he now keeping it a secret?

What do you mean, you don't know why? There's your answer.

He glanced to where Rory was standing next to the dresser he and Walt had dragged in from the house. She had navy blue towels she'd brought from the main house in her hands.

"You said you were a dog handler in the army?"

He swallowed. "Yeah."

She frowned. "What happened to the K9 you were paired with?"

"Well, for about a year I thought he'd died."

"But he hadn't, had he?" She held the towels against her chest. "Because he's right here isn't he, Mitch?"

"How did you figure it out?" *Ludicrous question, Sawicki.* Yeah, he deserved the you've-got-to-be-joking look she gave him.

"Sarge has been here a year. A full year. Where were you for the past year? Why has it taken you so long to come and see him?" She hugged the towels as if they would offer some protection.

"Because I thought he was dead," he spat out. Guilt assailed him. "We got separated during…during an attack. As much as I hated it, I had to accept he was gone."

He wanted to tell her the full story, but the words wouldn't come. He couldn't even name all the emotions that seemed to assail him all at once.

She shook her head in disbelief and set the towels on the dresser. "And you didn't bother to look for him?"

No, and that's my shame. "I was a little busy."

He'd been in and out of the hospital a few times during that year. Toxic imbedded fragments from shrapnel had become infected requiring treatment plus he'd been in several places for physical therapy.

"And now that you've found him?"

He opened his mouth and shut it again. What was he supposed to say?

"I see." She shook her head and walked to the door. "I hope you're not expecting me to hand over a dog that we've had for a full year. A full year."

"I know how long it's been. Do you think I—"

"And you're forgetting one important thing. Sarge belongs to Bowie. I don't care what sort of sob story you want to peddle. I am not giving away my brother's dog while he's put himself in harm's way serving his country."

"I had hoped to—"

"And Phoebe loves that dog. She would be devastated to lose him. I will not do that to her. I don't care what your excuse is for not coming sooner. Bowie never made Sarge's adoption and presence here a secret. Or did you wait for my brother to leave to come here?"

Mitch saw red. He'd always thought that was just

some turn of a phrase. But a red mist descended over his vision. "You want to know what I was doing for the past twelve months?"

She was already a good ten feet away from the bunkhouse, but she turned back. "I'm listening. Tell me what was so damn important."

He stepped outside and searched for calm so he could explain, but he couldn't find any calm. Nor could he find words, any words, couldn't form a coherent sentence or thought. Instead, he undid his belt, unbuttoned his pants and unzipped them.

This was wrong and unacceptable behavior, but he was past the point of caring. She'd practically accused him of willfully abandoning Sarge. And the thing was, maybe somewhere deep down in a place he refused to examine, he agreed with her. What kind of person did that make him? This was a dog who would have given his life for him; this was a dog who did give his leg for him, and Mitch had taken someone's word that he was dead. He didn't search for him. He gave up, lost in his own self-pity for all that time.

Guilt, rage and a whole host of feelings he couldn't even name made him continue. He gave a hard tug and let his pants drop. It didn't take much effort and they were pooled around his ankles.

"This," he pointed to his prosthetic, "this is what I was doing for the past year."

What the hell, Sawicki? Have you completely lost your ever-lovin' mind?

She lifted her gaze from his prosthetic leg to

meet his. He managed to hold her gaze for a few seconds before having to break away. Unable to tell if her shock was due to his rash actions or the reality of his injury. Or both. But did it really matter?

Suddenly mortified, he muttered a curse and bent over to grab his pants, yanked them back up and stomped off, heading for his truck. Why hadn't he simply rolled up his pant leg? Because that's what a sane man would have done. Why had her accusations made him incapable of rational thought?

Face it, he told himself, it wasn't just her accusations but her. His brain shed IQ points like a snake shedding its skin when he was with her.

He continued to put as much distance between them as quickly as he could. She'd be kicking him off the farm. And he didn't blame her. She might even get that deputy to escort him out of town, out of her life. Hers and Phoebe's. If Walt didn't get to him first. He snorted a mirthless laugh. Walt would want to tear him apart for scaring Rory. And he must have scared her with his anger and his actions. And he couldn't blame her.

Still in shock and trying to process all the emotions bubbling up in her, she stood unmoving, not even breathing, for several moments. When she finally turned, she saw Mitch heading for his Toyota and that spurred her into action.

"Wait," she called and scrambled to catch up with him. "Mitch, wait up."

He finally stopped and swung around to face

her. His cheeks stained with red. "Why? So you can kick my butt? Tell me to leave and not come back?"

"Why would I do that?" Yes, she was angry that he hadn't been honest, but his actions since arriving bespoke an honorable man buried somewhere under all that anger. He'd shown kindness and compassion with Phoebe and had bonded with Walt.

The fact he expected fury spoke volumes. He was probably angrier at himself than she was.

He shook his head. "I don't know, but let me give it a guess. I probably scared the—"

"Look, I admit to being startled, but you're not exactly scary. I know that probably goes against your Ranger persona and I'm sorry, but I don't see you as threatening. Should I?"

"I wouldn't physically hurt you or Phoebe or Walt, I swear." He stood watching her.

"There. That's settled and if I'm TSTL for not sending you packing, then so be it."

He frowned. "What the heck is TSTL?"

She smiled. "Too Stupid To Live."

"Ah. I'll make a guess and say that's from those books I see piled on your coffee table and end tables."

"Do you have a problem with my choice of reading material?"

"Absolutely not. My mother reads them too. She did her best to instill in me a love of reading."

"You make it sound as if she failed." And why where they talking about this? She didn't have an answer, but if it kept him from jumping into his truck and pealing out, she'd take it.

He shrugged. "Not completely. Although I confess my taste runs more to Crais or Baldacci than romance."

"I like them too, but lately much of my reading time has been spent with Phoebe and her owl book."

"Ah, yes, the owl book."

She laughed. "Already regretting that promise?"

"Nah, I found it rather fascinating. I didn't realize how much I didn't know about owls."

"Yeah, I'm fast becoming an expert too."

"We'll be a pair of ornithologists by the time we get to the end," he said.

"Sorry about that."

"It's not one of those little storybooks my mother read to me as a kid but I did enjoy what I've read so far."

Something shifted in the region of her heart as she tried to imagine Mitch as a little boy being read to by his mother. It helped melt away any residual true anger she may have been harboring, despite telling him she wasn't angry. She wondered if he was still close with his parents before smiling and saying, "I'm glad."

He tilted his head as he studied her, his eyes full of some undefinable emotion. "I still can't believe you're not angry with me."

"I never said I wasn't upset." Maybe she *was* one of those heroines she rolled her eyes at when they forgave the hero for his bad behavior in both books and movies.

"But I flashed you."

She laughed. "I don't know where you grew up but around these parts you have to actually show a girl some serious skin for it to be considered flashing. Heck, I've seen more at the lake when this guy I used to see around town was into his Speedo phase. Julian Bond. Yeah, that was his name."

He opened his mouth and she held up her hand. "Don't even ask," she said and shuddered. "I was still in high school so I considered him ancient and the image is still with me."

That earned her one of those lopsided grins. "So, if anger is out, what about appalled? Disgusted? Or any number of things you should be?"

"No. I'm not. I wish I had known before I started accusing you of abandoning Sarge, but I'm not angry or any of those other things. At least not anymore."

"Then what are you?"

"Annoyed you didn't tell me the truth, that you didn't trust me with what actually happened. But at the moment? Mostly curious. I want to know what happened to you over there. At least I assume it happened while you were deployed. And Sarge was involved."

"It did. A roadside bomb exploded, hitting the vehicle Sarge and I were riding in. Very cliché."

He might be downplaying whatever happened, but she knew he was still dealing with it, mentally and physically. She'd witnessed the anger and frustration that had been simmering in him, so decided to proceed gently with Mitch. "Is that when Sarge lost his leg too?"

"I have to assume so. I confess I was out of it most of the time. Luckily, they sent in PJs—those are pararescue jumpers. They're like battlefield EMTs. Anyway, I was helicoptered out. I asked about Sarge before the helo even lifted off the ground, but the PJ shook his head and apologized. And I made an assumption I never should have made. You're right. I don't deserve him."

"I don't think that's what I said and don't you say it either. I understand now why you thought he didn't make it."

"Once I had regained consciousness, I should have demanded answers."

"You must've been in a lot of pain." She hated to think about what he must've gone through.

"No excuse. They had me on plenty of painkillers most of the time."

"I'm not talking physical agony." She reached out and touched his arm. "I meant emotionally. You'd lost part of your leg and thought you'd lost your dog too."

"That doesn't excuse my behavior," he muttered, staring off into the distance, obviously lost battling his demons.

She squeezed his arm to bring him back to the present. "How about we go to the house? I have some oatmeal cookies, and I can make some coffee. Walt and Phoebe took Sarge to the dog park. They'll be gone for a bit."

Not waiting for a response, she began walking to the house. All the while castigating herself. What in the world made her think coffee and cookies would help in a situation like this? When a wounded warrior was still struggling to come to terms with the end of his career and a completely new life, back home in America? But it was the best thing she could think of.

She didn't turn around but kept walking. Would he join her? Or would he give up and leave. *Don't leave*, she begged silently. *I'm not ready to see you leave.*

Unable to stand the suspense any longer, she turned her head enough to see him in her peripheral vision. He stood in the same spot as if debating with himself. Decision evidently made, he caught up and fell into step beside her.

She started to slow her steps and he clicked his tongue in apparent disapproval. "Don't do that."

"Do what?" She turned her head all the way this time to allow herself to look at him full-on, trying to decipher the emotion lurking in his eyes.

He frowned. "You never once adjusted your steps with me before. Why are you doing it now?"

He sounded peeved and she regretted it, even if her change in gait had been an unconscious reaction. "I'm sorry. I didn't do it on purpose. Honest. Is that why you didn't want to tell me?"

"It might have been one of the reasons but mostly

because it wasn't something that came up in our conversations so far."

"Well, I didn't know what had happened to you until you told me."

They reached the back door that led to the kitchen via the mud room. He opened the door and held it for her. Although she didn't comment on his manners, she liked them. Having a gentleman around was pretty nice, made her feel special. She went into the mudroom and unzipped her light-weight jacket.

"Does the rubber band you wear on your wrist have anything to do with the amputation?"

He nodded and told her about the phantom feelings as they wiped their feet on the mat and hung their jackets on hooks attached to the paneled walls.

"Was phantom pain bothering you the first day you came here? When I upset you with my mothering comment?"

"My foot itched and I had left the band in the truck." He followed her into the kitchen. "And I angered you with my response, so I guess that made us even."

So, he had noticed her reaction. Why would that have given her butterflies in her stomach? She turned to look him in the eyes. "Frankly, mothering you was the last thing on my mind."

"Oh?" He lifted an eyebrow, his pale eyes shining with interest. "Do tell."

"I think the statement speaks for itself," she said. She wasn't trying to be mysterious, just hoping to get her riotous heartbeat under control. She went to the antique Hoosier cabinet, pulled out the tin of homemade cookies and set them on the butcher block kitchen island.

"Do you need help with anything?" he asked and went to the sink.

"No but thank you for offering."

He washed and dried his hands and stood on the other side of the island from her. After opening the tin, he grabbed a cookie. "Yum, homemade."

"Yeah, I've been experimenting trying to make some of my recipes a bit healthier. Swapping out some of the fat and sugar when I can."

"For Walt?"

"For all of us." She put a pod into the coffee maker and started it, using the task to allow her time to gather her thoughts.

"Does that include me?"

He bit into a cookie and chewed. "These aren't bad...for healthy cookies."

She turned around. "What's that supposed— *Oh*."

"Gotcha." He grinned and reached for another cookie. "So, you didn't tell me if this eating better at home plan of yours included me, your newest tenant."

She swallowed and turned back to fiddle with the coffee maker. Where was this conversation going? She was still trying to wrap her head around what had just happened and what that meant for them. "Do you *want* it to include you?"

"Yes."

That simple word, spoken with conviction, raised goose bumps on her arm. Did *she* want it to include him too? She set the mugs she'd gotten out on the counter.

"It's okay if you're not sure. I'm not—"

"Yes," she practically shouted and twirled around again to face him. "I want it to include you."

He leaned over the island and cupped her upturned face in his palms. He stared into her eyes. "That's good to know. Does this mean our date is still on?"

So, it really was a date? Her heart continued to beat erratically. How did she feel about that? Good. Damn good. "Yes. Unless you did that to get out of our date?"

He laughed, his breath warming her face. "A bit elaborate, wouldn't you say? Saying I changed my mind would have been a heck of a lot easier, not to mention way less embarrassing. Saying I changed my mind wouldn't have involved you seeing me in my skivvies."

"But it was such a nice sight," she said dreamily.

He gave her a look that shouted disbelief. "As I recall, you said it was very unimpressive."

"Oh my goodness," she laid her hand on her chest, "did I say that?"

"You certainly implied it. You compared me to some old guy at the beach in a Speedo."

"Well, shame on me. I hope this won't jeopardize our date for pancakes at Aunt Polly's."

"It'll take more than that to get out of it," he promised, all the while bringing himself closer.

"Are you doing that so you don't disappoint Phoebe?"

"Is that what you think?"

"Frankly, I don't know what to think. I—I didn't even know if it was even a real date."

"I'd like it to be. What about you?"

She swallowed. Putting herself out there wouldn't be easy, but she didn't want to let this opportunity with Mitch slip through her hands because she did nothing. And Phoebe took to him like a duck to water too. "I'd like it to be."

He leaned closer; his palms still cupped around her face. She knew in that moment he was going to kiss her. The first man to do so since the divorce. She gazed into his green eyes and drew closer, welcoming his kiss. A kiss she'd thought about ever since she'd discovered him at her door.

Chapter Nine

"I'm glad," he whispered as he brought his lips closer.

His breath blew warm on her face, and she brought her hands up, laying her open palms on his chest. She felt the thud of his heart under her hands. Hers was beating just as fast.

Finally, his lips brushed across hers, lightly at first. Those lips she'd been wondering about were firm but gentle. So gentle. She sighed, parting her lips. His tongue swept in to brush against hers and she groaned.

Hot liquid started draining from the coffee maker, sizzling and splashing when it hit the bottom.

Mitch pulled away and reached over, grabbing

the mug she had set on the counter and pushing it under the stream of coffee.

She reached for his hand. "Oh no! Did you burn yourself?"

He flexed his hand and winced. "It's okay. I'll survive."

"This was all my fault." She pulled him over to the sink and turned on the cold-water tap.

"I think we were both…a bit…distracted," he said and let her put his hand under the running water.

She met his gaze and he raised an eyebrow. "You're not mothering me, are you?"

"I'm caring for you," she corrected. Would she never live that comment down? She'd been concerned for him. Was that so wrong? "Would you like some aloe salve for it?"

"Or you could just kiss it and make it better," he suggested, his dark eyebrows bobbed mischievously.

"Sorry, but I'm afraid that crosses the line into mothering territory," she said.

He shut the tap off and patted a towel over his hand to dry it. "Maybe it's a good thing I'm such a rule breaker then."

"Regretfully, I'm not."

He heaved an exaggerated sigh and hung the towel back up. "Just my luck."

He didn't take a seat at the table so neither did she, instead opting to set her filled mug on the island. She stood facing him and placed napkins alongside the cookie tin. Selecting a cookie, she broke it in half and set the pieces on the napkin. She couldn't get the kiss out of her mind but decided to leave it alone…for now. She'd wanted it to go on so much longer than that brief embrace.

"Why would you think I wouldn't want to go out with you?" she asked instead but didn't give him a chance to respond before continuing, "If you think it's because you flashed me, think again. I was married. I've seen a man in his underwear before. And frankly, your boxer briefs are pretty basic. Not all that sexy."

Liar, liar, pants on fire! She would never have thought simple black cotton underwear could be so sexy. But that was because she hadn't seen Mitch wearing them.

He had just taken a sip and started making sputtering choking sounds before setting the cup back down. "That's your takeaway from my little performance? Are you going to ignore the elephant in the room?"

"I guess you're talking about the fact you have a prosthetic." She raised an eyebrow as she studied him. "You think that would bother me? I should be insulted that you would think so."

"I'm sorry but it bothered my ex-fiancée so much she called off our engagement."

Her stomach had tightened when he mentioned a onetime fiancée. He had loved someone enough to want to marry them. She hated that thought as much as she hated that of him lying in a pool of blood on a battlefield. But she had no right to any jealousy because she'd been married before. Why was that any different?

Because deep down she knew she hadn't loved Curt enough to forgive him for financially ruining them. Damn, but that made her sound mercenary, but it had been the lies she couldn't forgive. They'd married because she'd gotten pregnant with Phoebe, and she'd loved Curt the best she could. But that obviously wasn't enough to save the marriage when times got tough. If her husband had really cared enough for his wife and child, he wouldn't have risked everything they had built—everything they had put aside for Phoebe's future—on what amounted to a whim. She couldn't love a man who was that selfish.

She pushed the memories and the jealousy aside. Mitch had said *ex-fiancée*, so it didn't mean anything now. Right? "Then she must have been a fool. You don't have to talk about it if you don't want to."

"It's okay." He shrugged as if he was indifferent, but the tension he carried in those broad shoulders showed. "We wanted different things and she informed me that our relationship would be proceeding without me."

She suspected his flippant comment was a way of hiding the hurt. "So, when you said you wanted different things…"

He snorted a mirthless laugh. "Yeah, she wanted someone with two good legs."

She tried to swallow past the lump in her throat.

How could anyone think this wonderful man was anything less? "I reiterate, she was a fool."

"Have you considered that maybe *you* are?" he asked quietly and took a bite of his cookie and washed it down with a sip of coffee.

His gaze finally met hers, defiance lurking in its depth. She wanted to wrap him in her arms but feared rejection. Instead, she lifted her chin in her own gesture of defiance. "A fool for believing in you? Why would you say that?"

"Do you have any idea how my life has changed since this happened?"

"No, but I didn't know you before, so I have nothing to compare it to. As for right now, you seem to get around perfectly fine. I had no idea you were an amputee until you dropped your pants."

"But you suspected something."

"What do you—oh, are you talking about when I asked you if something was wrong? I saw you rubbing your thigh as if you were in pain. I meant what I said…well, except the part about mothering you. As I said, that was the last thing from my mind," she admitted.

"There are nerves remaining which still send signals to my brain, so I get sensations."

She hated the thought he might be in continued pain. "Those signals…is that what causes phantom pain I've heard about?"

"Yeah, and other sensations like my foot itching."

"Oh no. Is there anything you can do about other it than the rubber band?"

"There's medication, but I don't like the side effects. I prefer the rubber band approach. Quick but usually effective."

She winced.

Before she thought of anything to say, he lifted a shoulder in a careless shrug. "It can be better than having an itch you can't scratch."

"I remember when I had an epidural when I gave birth to Phoebe. Before it wore off completely, I started getting cramps in my legs because it felt as though I was in the fetal position from when they gave me the shot. The nurse showed me my legs were out straight, but my brain was telling me otherwise. Is it like that?"

"Yeah, I suppose that comes the closest."

"But I was lucky because it wore off eventually. Will it be like that for you?"

"I'm told that most—about seventy-five percent—subsides after the first two years. So, only a year to go. More or less."

"I'm so sorry," she said, which was a totally inadequate thing to say. Or maybe not. She knew from experience that sometimes sorry was the only thing you could say.

He had picked his cup up but set it back without taking a sip. "I don't need—or want—pity. From anyone."

Though it was unspoken, she heard the implied "especially you" in his statement. Yeah, resisting her urge to hug him had been a good call. "I wasn't offering pity. I can be empathetic without pitying you so don't snap at me."

"Sorry." He visibly relaxed and smiled. "Or should I say, yes, ma'am."

"And don't *ma'am* me either. I'm not that old." She tried to sound offended but knew she'd failed when he grinned.

"So I noticed." He leaned across the table toward her. "I honestly didn't mean to flash you like that. It just… I felt so angry and helpless, and I reacted harshly in that moment."

"I'm sorry if I made you angry. I shouldn't have harangued you like that." Why had she? Was it because she wanted to believe in him? She'd wanted an explanation she could accept and go on believing in him. Well, she'd gotten one…maybe even more than she'd expected.

"You had every right to question me. I wasn't upset with you or at you. I guess I'm still working at accepting what's happened to me. In the beginning I felt sorry for myself, but when I thought about my friends who'd died, or the one who did survive but with a traumatic brain injury, I realized feeling sorry for myself wasn't doing any good and it was like thumbing my nose at their sacrifices."

He leaned over the butcher block until he was close enough that she could smell coffee on his breath. She reached across the small square to put her hands on his chest, over his heart. She inched closer until their bodies were close enough that his lips could brush across hers. His lips were firm but gentle. More, she wanted more. Their positions with the island between them made the whole thing as awkward as hell. But she didn't want to break away to change positions. And it appeared Mitch didn't either, because neither one of them stopped.

"Mommy? What are you and Mr. Mitch doing?"

At the sound of Phoebe's voice, they sprang apart.

"I...uh, we..." Rory sputtered. Talk about embarrassing. She was pretty sure her face was crimson by now.

Walt followed Phoebe through the door. "Sorry if we interrupted...something."

Oh dear God, it was like being a teenager and getting caught necking. "You didn't...we...uh, we..." She fumbled for an explanation.

"Rory had something in her eye, and I was checking to see if she'd gotten it out," Mitch said, his voice steady and matter of fact.

Sarge charged across the kitchen, his nails clicking on the floor, and went straight to his water dish and noisily slurped water.

"Of course." Walt snort-laughed. "The old something in my eye trick."

"What did you get in your eye, Mommy? Did it hurt? Why is it a trick?" Phoebe came to stand in front of her full of concern until she spotted the open cookie tin. "Is you and Mr. Mitch having cookies? Can I have one too?"

"Sure, why not. Cookies all around," Rory said

FREE BOOKS GIVEAWAY

2 FREE ROMANCE BOOKS!

2 FREE WHOLESOME ROMANCE BOOKS!

GET UP TO FOUR FREE BOOKS & TWO FREE GIFTS WORTH OVER $20!

We pay for everything!

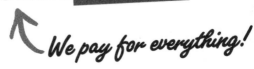

See Details Inside

Dear Reader,

I am writing to announce the launch of a huge **FREE BOOK GIVEAWAY**... and to let you know that YOU are entitled to choose up to FOUR fantastic books that WE pay for.

Try **Harlequin® Special Edition** books featuring comfort and strength in the support of loved ones and enjoying the journey no matter what life throws your way.

Try **Harlequin® Heartwarming™ Larger-Print** books featuring uplifting stories where the bonds of friendship, family and community unite.

Or TRY BOTH!

In return, we ask just one favor: Would you please participate in our brief Reader Survey? We'd love to hear from you.

This FREE BOOKS GIVEAWAY means that your introductory shipment is completely free, even the shipping! If you decide to continue, you can look forward to curated monthly shipments of brand-new books from your selected series, always at a discount off the cover price! Plus you can cancel any time. Who could pass up a deal like that?

Sincerely

Pam Powers

Pam Powers
For Harlequin Reader Service

Complete the survey below and return it today to receive up to **4 FREE BOOKS** and **FREE GIFTS** guaranteed!

FREE BOOKS GIVEAWAY
Reader Survey

1

Do you prefer stories with happy endings?

○ YES   ○ NO

2

Do you share your favorite books with friends?

○ YES   ○ NO

3

Do you often choose to read instead of watching TV?

○ YES   ○ NO

YES! Please send me my Free Rewards, consisting of **2 Free Books** from each series I select and **Free Mystery Gifts**. I understand that I am under no obligation to buy anything, no purchase necessary see terms and conditions for details.

❑ **Harlequin® Special Edition** (235/335 HDL GRM5)
❑ **Harlequin® Heartwarming™ Larger-Print** (161/361 HDL GRM5)
❑ **Try Both** (235/335 & 161/361 HDL GRNH)

FIRST NAME | LAST NAME

ADDRESS

APT.# | CITY

STATE/PROV. | ZIP/POSTAL CODE

EMAIL ❑ Please check this box if you would like to receive newsletters and promotional emails from Harlequin Enterprises ULC and its affiliates. You can unsubscribe anytime.

SE/HW-122-FBG22_SE/HW-122-FBGVR

weakly, stepping back from the counter—and Mitch.

Sarge left the water dish and came to sit in front of Rory as if he understood she was the dispenser of the goodies.

"Sorry but I wasn't including you. These have raisins," Rory told him, and he whined.

Join the club, she thought. She felt like whining when she thought about her and Mitch getting interrupted. Now that she knew how those lips felt on hers, she wanted more. A whole *lot* more.

"Mr. Mitch, did you know doggies can't have raisins? We has to be very caw…caw— What's that word?" Phoebe asked.

"Cautious," he supplied. "It's probably best not to give him any people food."

"That's 'xactly what Mommy says. Did she tell you that too? Is that what you was talking about? Can I have some milk with my cookies?"

Rory met Mitch's gaze and smiled. He seemed to be taking all Phoebe's questions in stride. His ex must have been extremely shallow to let someone as caring as Mitch slip through her fingers. If that woman were here now, she'd give her a piece of her mind. No, wait. *Be glad she's not here because that would mean Mitch might not be here either.* So hurray for the shallow ex.

"Mommy? Did you forget my milk?"

Phoebe's question brought her out of her reverie. She took the jug out of the refrigerator and, turning back, she caught her uncle contemplating her. She raised an eyebrow at him and he simply grinned.

"Grandpa G, why is Mommy getting something in her eye a trick?" Phoebe said again.

Now it was her turn to grin at Walt.

"I was just joking, Munchkin. How about you pass your old grandpa a cookie?"

A few minutes later, everyone seated at the kitchen table, she glanced around. Phoebe was eating cookies and drinking milk, Mitch petting the dog and Walt sipping coffee. The sights, sounds, aromas warmed her, and she reveled in her contentment. She didn't know what the future held for everyone in this room, but she'd savor this perfect moment.

Later that evening as Mitch was making his way back to the bunkhouse, Walt accompanied him, saying he needed to check on something in the barn. Mitch suspected by Rory's expression that she knew her uncle had ulterior motives. Probably wanted to have a chat similar to the one that deputy had conducted. It didn't come as a surprise, and he was okay with it. After all, he'd been caught kissing the man's niece.

Sarge came running up alongside them.

"How'd you escape the women?" Walt asked the dog as Sarge joined them.

Sarge woofed and looked up at both of them with a huge canine smile. Spotting something, the dog loped over and came back with a stick in his mouth.

"So, you wanna play, do you?" Mitch asked and took the stick, tossing it as far as he could ahead of them.

Walt pulled a cigar from his pocket and ran it back and forth under his nose, sniffing as he did. "I'd offer you one, but I only have the one with me."

Mitch waved his hand. "I'm good."

"I sneak them when I can. She doesn't approve," Walt said and jerked his head toward the house.

Mitch huffed out a laugh. "I think she disapproves because she's worried about your health."

Walt took a small gadget out of his pocket and snipped the end off the cigar.

Mitch hitched his chin at the gadget. "You a serious smoker?"

Sarge came back and dropped the stick at Mitch's feet. He picked it up and tossed it again.

Walt lit the cigar and stuck it in his mouth. "Not as serious as I used to be. Rory's been on my case since the heart attack. That girl fusses too much, even though she's pretty much a daughter to me. Takes the world on her shoulders sometimes, especially after her divorce. She means well, but I can't stand someone hovering like I'm some invalid."

"Tell me about it."

Walt gave him a sharp look. "She's not trying to mother you too, is she?"

Mitch chuckled. At least they'd gotten that much cleared up before the others had returned. "No, I was thinking of my own mother."

"Losing a leg, even half of one, is no small deal."

At first, Walt's comment surprised Mitch, but he soon realized the older guy would have found out when he had his military record checked out. Even with HIPAA and all that, it wasn't hard to find out about the incident, who had been hurt, and how badly.

Sarge came over again with the stick but instead of tossing it, Mitch looked to Walt. "Do you limit his exercise...you know, because of the leg?"

"Some, but you're good with a few more tosses."

Mitch threw the stick again and the dog raced after it. "He doesn't seem to miss it."

"Nah. Animals live in the moment. Maybe that's good advice for some people too."

Mitch nodded but didn't respond. They stood together, just enjoying the warm spring weather, Mitch amazed at the stars in the night sky without all the light pollution he was accustomed too and Walt happily exhaling with the simple pleasure of a good cigar.

Walt gently blew the smoke from his mouth. "I'm not exactly sure what's going on with you and my niece."

"We're getting to know one another," Mitch told him, but the truth was, he wasn't exactly sure himself what they were doing. Although that answer seemed the most honest he could give.

"Is that what you're calling it?"

"Well, I—"

"It's okay, I'm not warning you off. She's a grown woman and capable of making her own decisions." He stubbed out the cigar. "But she's been through a lot, and so has Phoebe. So no funny business. You treat both of them right and you and I will get along."

"You mean her parents? That must have really affected her." What was Walt's definition of funny business? He'd ask, but he was afraid he might not like the answer. If things proceeded as they were, he and Rory just might engage in some of that so-called funny business. He also wondered what Rory had been through during her marriage. Had that guy done something? Mitch's fingers curled into a fist at the thought.

"Yeah, she and the boy were devastated by the loss of their parents, and each has reacted in their own ways."

"How did Rory react?" Mitch asked but shook his head. Damn, that might not be any of his business and he said as much to Walt.

"In my opinion she married too young but I couldn't talk her out of it. I did my best but I think she craved a family of her own."

"Her ex-husband didn't…?" He cautioned himself against overstepping but the words were out before he could stop them.

Walt shook his head. "Nah. Nothing like that. They simply couldn't handle the strain of their failed business and financial troubles. At least that's my take on it."

Mitch nodded. "Each sibling reacted differently

to the same tragedy. Like Bowie opting for danger and saving the world?"

"He's well trained."

Mitch knew Bowie was in the Navy so he put two and two together. "A SEAL?"

Walt gave him a look. "You know we're not supposed to discuss it with outsiders."

Outsiders? Is that what he was? As much as he hated the thought, he understood he didn't have the right to know. Not yet.

Not yet? If the fact he was thinking in terms of something much more with Rory, something that might even be permanent, didn't send him packing, he wasn't sure what would.

"You got a problem with that, son?" Walt was asking.

Mitch shook his head to get it back in the game. "No, sir. There was a lot of stuff I couldn't even talk about with my mother."

Walt nodded. "Are you and her close?"

Mitch thought about how he couldn't wait to pack up and leave because he'd felt smothered. That thought caused a sharp pain of regret and grief. How could he blame his mother for her reaction when he himself had freaked out over his amputation? "It was just the two of us growing up. Apparently, my father decided before I was even born that being a parent wasn't for him."

"That's rough."

"My mom's a strong, wonderful woman. I

credit her with giving me the confidence to make it through Ranger training."

"Have you ever told her that?"

"What are you? My conscience?" he grumbled good naturedly. He might have been joking, but if he were honest with himself, his conscience had been itching since he'd cut short his last visit.

Walt faced him. "Should I be?"

"She fussed over me after I was released from the hospital."

"And you didn't want to be fussed over?"

"No more than you want to be." Not like that wasn't messed up or anything.

Walt nodded. "I get that, but if we want them in our lives, I'm thinking we need to put up with some of that kind of loving."

Walt didn't wait for an answer but whistled for the dog who was inspecting some smells near the barn. "C'mon, dog, say your good-night. We need to get back."

Long after he'd left Walt and gone into the bunkhouse, Mitch thought about Walt's words. He then picked up his phone and called his mom.

Chapter Ten

Rory checked her reflection in the mirror one last time before leaving her bedroom the next morning. She'd chosen to wear a simple sleeveless shift with a sapphire-blue geometric pattern against a white background. The dress fell to just above her knees and she paired it with a pair of flat, casual sandals. She'd fallen in love with the dress when she'd spotted it in the window of a consignment shop over a year ago. This was the first time she'd worn it, though.

She smoothed her hand down the front of the garment. This might not be like a normal date, but tell that to the butterflies tap-dancing in her stomach. Halfway down the hall she hesitated. Would Mitch think she was overdressed? Would he think she was reading too much into this breakfast date—despite their kisses? Pushing her shoulders back, she descended the stairs. She loved the dress and was going to wear it. Who knew when or even if she'd get another chance? He'd have to deal if he didn't like it.

She walked into the living room where Phoebe was already waiting, looking out the front window and hopping from one foot to the other in impatience.

Phoebe stilled her movements when she spotted Rory. "Mommy, you looks bootiful. What about me? Do I look bootiful too?"

"Very beautiful. That looks like a dress a real princess would wear," Rory assured her daughter, who was wearing a flowered-print dress with a smocked bodice.

"Like the princess in the picture?"

Rory smiled and nodded, assuming Phoebe was referring to the picture she'd seen of Princess Charlotte on a magazine cover. Once Phoebe learned the little girl was a real-life princess, she had slept with the photo next to her bed. Rory had searched online to find an affordable dress similar to the one the young royal was wearing.

"He's here." Phoebe ran to the door and swung it open before Mitch could even knock. "Mr. Mitch, do I look pretty? Do I look like a princess in this dress? Mommy bought it for me so I could look like the one in the picture."

"Phoebe, please, let Mr. Mitch catch his breath."

As if in deference to their date, Mitch wore khakis with a neatly pressed dark blue button-down shirt. She had nothing against the clothes he normally wore but it was as if she was seeing a new side to him. And she liked it. A lot. What had he looked like in his dress uniform? Did he have a chest full of ribbons like Bowie?

"I think she's the one who needs to catch her breath." Mitch chuckled and met Rory's gaze.

No, I think I'm the one who will need to catch their breath if you keep looking at me like that.

Phoebe danced around. "I've never been on a date before. Have you, Mr. Mitch?"

"A few but none as special as this one," he assured her.

Mitch shifted from one foot to the other as he waited with Rory and Phoebe by the little sign at Aunt Polly's that asked customers to wait to be seated. Was it his imagination or was everyone in the place watching them? Of course they were and he shouldn't be surprised. This was a small town and considering that practically everyone greeted Rory and Phoebe as if they were lifelong friends. And they probably were, he laughed to himself. This breakfast promised to be the talk of the town. Not that he really cared. He was just happy to be with both of them. If anyone had any reason to worry about talk, it was Rory. She lived here and was starting a new business venture. He was just passing through…right?

The waitress, the same one he had the one other time he'd come, led them to their seats. He laughed when he saw it was the same booth.

Trudi turned and grinned, obviously sharing the humor in the situation. "I saved it special for you."

"Why did you save the seats?" Phoebe asked Trudi as she climbed into the booth. "Did Mr. Mitch tell you we was coming?"

"No, but I saw you coming," the waitress said.

"How did you see us?" Phoebe patted the empty spot next to her. "Can you sit next to me, Mr. Mitch?"

He would have preferred sitting next to Rory, but he smiled and accepted his fate, slipping onto the seat next to Phoebe.

"I looked out that window and saw you coming," Trudi pointed toward the booth and the window.

"Oh." Phoebe seemed very disappointed at the simple explanation.

"Cheer up, Princess. We don't allow long faces here at Aunt Polly's," the waitress said as she handed them menus.

Mitch leaned toward Phoebe. "I see everyone in Loon Lake knows about your royal status."

Phoebe giggled and nodded. His heart constricted at her sweet reaction, and he wondered if he was already too attached to the child. If he wasn't planning on sticking around, would it be harmful to get so close to Phoebe—and then leave?

Mitch looked at Rory. "And do they know about your royal status?"

She rolled her eyes at him.

"Hey, being seen with Sleeping Beauty is a big deal for me," he joked.

"What about me? Am I a big deal too?" Phoebe sat on her knees and placed her elbows on the table.

"Absolutely," Mitch told her seriously.

Phoebe rested her chin on her cupped palm and stared at him. "Mr. Mitch?"

"Yes, Princess?"

"Can we go on an un-chap-in-ded date?"

"I'm not sure what that means, Princess," he said with a grin because the fact he sounded like Phoebe wasn't lost on him. "Could you possibly mean un-chaperoned?"

"Yeah, that's the word," she nodded her head vigorously.

"Phoebe, where do you get these things from?" Rory groaned, color rushing to her cheeks.

"That's what I heard Grandpa G tell Mr. Ogle when we went to the park. He said Mommy and Mr. Mitch would be going on one of those kind of dates soon. But I don't know what that word means."

Trudi came back with a coffee pot and empty mugs. "Are you folks ready to order or should I give you a few more minutes to decide?"

"Depends on what we're deciding," Rory muttered and buried her reddened face in the menu.

Mitch laughed; he couldn't help himself. He'd been so concerned himself over whether or not this could be considered a date. Now that he was here, it didn't matter what anyone labeled it, because he was enjoying being with Rory and Phoebe. And he didn't care who saw them or knew it. Yeah, they'd be the talk of the town, but it was worth it to spend time with Rory.

Mitch glanced up at the waitress with her pencil poised above her order pad and winked. "What would you call it, Trudi, when I show up with the two prettiest ladies in town?"

Trudi licked her lips. "Luck? Mistaken identity? Chloroform?"

Rory was still hiding behind the menu, but he distinctly heard a chortling sound coming from the other side of the plastic-covered pages.

"Hey, hey," Mitch said, feigning outrage. Did joking with the waitress mean he was already on his way to becoming part of this town? Was that what he wanted?

Phoebe patted his arm. "It's okay, Mr. Mitch, Mommy and Miz Trudi aren't wearing mad faces."

Mitch's heart melted at the sincerity in Phoebe's tone. How could anyone resist her? Or her mother, for that matter? "Thank you, Princess."

"You're welcome. What's color foam?"

Mitch looked to the waitress. "Yes, Ms. Trudi, what is that?"

"It means I'm going to bring you some special crayons and pages to color while everyone decides what they want to eat."

"Mr. Mitch already said he's gonna let me pick out pancakes for him cuz I know the best ones."

"Well, okay then, I'll take your orders now," Trudi said, her pencil poised over her order pad.

Mitch followed Phoebe's advice and ordered the

carrot cake and walnut pancakes and a side of bacon. After taking their orders, Trudi fished around in the pocket of her apron and handed Phoebe a box of crayons.

Phoebe entertained herself by coloring and keeping up a running commentary on the owls she was drawing.

"You really know a lot about owls. Are you sure you're not an ornithologist already?" Mitch asked.

Phoebe giggled. "I'm not old enough to go to school yet."

She went back to concentrating on her pictures and Mitch looked across the table to meet Rory's gaze. She reached across and lightly touched his arm and mouthed the words *thank you* to him. Although unsure of what she was thanking him for, he nodded in response. Her pretty eyes softened, sending warmth radiating throughout his body. He could plan his future around that look and—

Whoa! Where had that come from? What in the world was he thinking? *Remember your plan for a selfish future*, he told himself but couldn't help meeting her gaze once more.

Mitch noticed movement and turned to see the deputy heading their way.

Phoebe spotted him too. "Hello, Dep-a-ty Cooper."

Deputy Cooper smiled and nodded. "Hello, Miss Phoebe. Rory."

Cooper nodded his head in acknowledgment of Mitch. "Sawicki."

"Deputy. As you can see, I brought protection with me today."

Cooper chuckled. "I can see that."

Trudi slid up beside him with a tray loaded with plates of food. "Are you here harassing my customers again? And while they're on a date. Shame on you."

"Sorry for the intrusion but I wanted to say hi and I'm here because Meg is craving cinnamon scones again."

Trudi set the tray down and raised an eyebrow. "Meg is having cravings?"

Cooper held his hands up, palms out and vigorously shook his head. "I'm not saying another word."

"I'll bag some up as soon as I've finished here," Trudi said and made a zipper motion across her lips.

"Be sure to tell Meg Phoebe and I said hi," Rory told Cooper.

"Will do. Have a good…" His lips twitching, Cooper's gaze landed on Mitch before he continued, "breakfast date."

Mitch accepted the inevitable. The whole town knew this was a date. But strangely, he was good with that.

Rory wasn't sure how she felt about this being a *real* date. Was that even possible with your daughter in tow? Glancing over the tabletop at Mitch as he smiled and said something to Phoebe about owls, the hairs on the back of her neck stood up. A lock of dark hair had fallen over his forehead and her fingers itched to brush it back in place.

No more denials, she told herself sternly. *You're starting to fall for the guy.* Was that a bad thing? She gave an inward sigh as she weighed her options. She could embrace it while he was here or she could protect herself by pushing him away. Would she be taking the chance at missing out on something good by nipping this in the bud? Or was she falling too soon, too fast for a man whose departure could destabilize Phoebe's life—and her own?

A week had passed since her breakfast date with Mitch. He hadn't asked her out again and she was doing her best not to read anything into it. After all, they saw one another on a daily basis. He'd even joined them for meals a few times.

Whenever he declined her invitations, she didn't press or demand an explanation. Was it because she was afraid he simply didn't want to spend time with her? If that was the case, maybe she didn't want to know. Or could he still be hung up on his ex? Or maybe he was one of those people who craved alone time.

Denial much, Rory?

This morning she and Mitch were working on the interior of the prefabricated henhouse he'd put together with Walt's help. They'd ended up with one meant to be a henhouse, so the modifications were kept to a minimum. She guessed the availability of those had to do with the popularity of raising chickens these days.

Mitch attached roosting perches while she filled the completed nesting boxes with straw.

"Maybe I should make some curtains to put on the windows," she said as she made sure the straw was evenly distributed.

"Yeah, right," he said and laughed.

Okay, maybe she should have kept that thought to herself.

He set the hammer down. "You're serious."

She started to duck her head but raised her chin instead. "It's my henhouse so I can do as I please."

"You're right." He picked the hammer back up and continued nailing. "I'm sorry. I didn't mean to disparage your efforts."

"But?" She put her hands on her hips but couldn't prevent her lips from twitching with the need to smile. Curtains in a henhouse was a bit over the top.

"Do you really think the hens will care?"

She shook her head. "All right I confess it was something I saw online and thought it looked cute but you're right. I don't think they serve a practical purpose."

"Unless, of course, you know something I don't. I'm from Chicagoland. We got our eggs from the supermarket."

"Do you miss Chicago?" Did he have plans to go back permanently?

He rubbed his chin. "Not really. It's nice when I go back to see my mom and I can see, do and eat familiar things but it's not like I'm pining for it."

"Was your ex from the same area?"

"Yeah, we met in school."

Is that why he was here instead of there? Was

he afraid of running into her? If so, then maybe he still had feelings for her.

"Are you and she still—"

"What? No! We're definitely through."

"Sounds like she hurt you."

He expelled a breath. "Now that I look back, I think my pride took the brunt of the hit instead of my heart."

"But you must've loved her if you were engaged," she said.

"I thought I did but looking back, I'm thinking it was one of those fires that burns hot but doesn't last."

"It lasted long enough for you to promise to spend the rest of your lives together," she persisted, wondering why he was downplaying the entire thing. Was he in denial because he still cared? The last thing she wanted to do was fall for some guy hung up on someone else. With one relationship mistake behind her, she didn't relish making another.

"Which was a mistake," he said.

She stiffened, thinking he had read her mind.

"Considering my deployments, we basically had a long-distance relationship," he continued, seemingly oblivious of her inner turmoil.

"Those can be hard to maintain," she said in as neutral of tone as she could manage.

"Or it was easy to overlook certain problems," he said. "What's between you and me is different."

Of course it was different. She was a single mother trying to eek out a living on a farm not some some leggy blonde who—

"Don't," he said.

She blinked. "Don't what?"

"I can see the wheels turning inside that brain of yours and don't like where it's going."

"How can you possibly know what I'm thinking?" she asked, not wanting him to know what she was thinking. She wasn't so self-effacing that she wanted to point out that she might come up lacking in a comparison with his ex.

"Rory," he said in a chiding tone. "You telegraph your thoughts onto your face."

"I thought I wore my heart on my sleeve?"

"I'm not sure I ever said that but…" he reached out and touched a tender finger to her bottom lip, "you do that too."

He cupped her chin in his hand before she could form a response. "Look at me and believe me when I say that's a refreshing change."

"Oh, I'm a change all right. I've seen a picture of your fiancée, Mitch." Oh no! The words had tumbled out before she could stop them. She nibbled on her bottom lip.

He scowled but something lit up his eyes as he watched her worrying her lower lip. "You have? How? Where?"

"Well… I…" she swallowed. "I *may* have Googled you and some, uh, some pictures of the two of you *may* have come up."

"Uh-huh."

"Hey, in my defense, I knew nothing about you and you were going to be around my daughter."

Which was the truth. Just not all of it. She'd also be curious on a personal level…just for her own sake.

He stroked the pad of his thumb across her lower lip and she felt the reverberations of that light touch all the way to the tips of her toes.

"Don't compare yourself to her. She doesn't have your strength. You're beautiful inside and out."

She swallowed, drinking in the compliment. "But I thought she was the one to break it off."

"She was and I know what you're getting at and it wasn't like that. You want to know how I felt after I got over the pointless pride thing? Relief."

"But if you hadn't gotten injured, you may very well be married to her. You might have been very happy together."

What are you doing, Rory?

Why couldn't she just accept the compliment and move on, change the subject?

"We might still be together, but I'm not so sure about the happy part. She showed her true colors after my injury. Don't get me wrong, I'm not blaming her."

"But she should have stuck by you, no matter what."

"If I was having trouble accepting my new reality, why should I have expected her to?" he asked.

"Because if she loved you enough to want to marry you, she should have been there for you," she insisted.

"Like you were there for your husband?" he snapped.

His volley of words hit its mark. Was this why she hadn't let up? Because she was seeing herself in his ex and she was afraid he would too? But if that was the case, she should have shut up and she hadn't. Did she want him to see her as she was, flaws and all?

Mitch shook his head at himself in self-disgust. What the hell was wrong with him? He never should have said something so hurtful. He didn't know what the problems were in her marriage other than what Walt had told him. According to Walt, Rory had married too young and financial troubles took their toll.

So what if she'd hit a nerve? That was *his* problem, not hers. But that was genuinely the case here, as opposed to the way he'd insisted to himself over and over in the first days after the breakup. He was more than the lower half of his left leg, but in the beginning he'd had trouble believing that himself. He would have denied it but in his mind much of his identity, his worth, was tied up in his being a Ranger. He'd known that as a profession it had an expiration date. The human body could only be pushed so far as the years took their toll. But damn it, he'd wanted to choose when it ended. An artificial limb had not been a part of his life plans. He'd lost more than his foot in the blast. But he hadn't lost his humanity and had no business in taking it out on Rory.

Pushing his fingers through his hair, he realized

he was standing alone as Rory disappeared around the corner of the barn.

"Rory, wait," he called and hurried after her.

He reached out and grabbed her arm, holding tight when she tried to shake him off. "I'm sorry. I shouldn't have said that."

"Then why did you?"

"Because I'm an ass," he said and dropped his hold on her arm.

"You won't get any arguments from me."

He winced. "You hit a nerve and I reacted."

"You think?"

He sighed. "You're not going to make this easy, are you?"

"Should I?"

"No." He reached out and took her hands in each of his and lightly squeezed. "I'm sorry."

"I guess you hit a nerve with me too," she admitted. "I still feel guilty for not being able to make my marriage work."

"I'm sure you didn't give up at the first sign of trouble."

"I'm not so sure about that." She heaved a sigh. "Maybe that's why I was so harsh talking about your ex. I saw myself in her."

He might not be the most enlightened guy but he didn't want her thinking poorly about herself if he could help it. "Some relationships can weather bad things happening and others can't. I've worked on moving past placing all the blame on my ex. It's taken me a while to come to terms with my amputation, I can't blame her if she couldn't. And maybe I needed to work through this new reality on my own. Or she was on a different timeline."

"I did try to make things work between us and…" Her voice trailed off as she met his gaze.

He trailed a finger down her cheek. "And you didn't want me thinking you were like my ex? Bailing at the first sign of trouble?"

"Something like that, yeah."

"I don't think that," he told her and just let himself get lost in her eyes. He had to clear his throat before he could continue. "Someone very wise once told me that just because a relationship ends doesn't mean it failed. Maybe it had run its course."

"And who said that?"

"My mother," he confessed, wondering what that bit of information would do to his man card.

"Gotta love a guy who listens to their mother," she said with a smile.

"Oh yeah?"

He leaned over and kissed her, sighing when their lips touched and feeling as if he'd finally come home.

Loon Lake might not have been a place he'd visited before but no matter what happened in the future, he would always have a soft spot in his heart for this place and its people.

Especially its people. He deepened the kiss, only pulling away when they heard Walt's pick up coming up the driveway.

Chapter Eleven

Mitch glanced up as he made his way toward the barn after a night of tossing and turning. One look toward the eastern sky had him stopping in his tracks. The predawn sky was awash in pink and orange.

"Gorgeous, isn't it?"

At the sound of the hushed question, Mitch turned around. Rory was approaching the barn. He nodded and put his hands in his pockets. Not so much to warm them from the slight chill in the air but to avoid the temptation to reach for her.

Despite the early hour, she appeared to be dressed for work in faded, torn jeans and a plaid flannel shirt, her hair pulled back. She shouldn't look sexy in that outfit but the muscles in his gut tightened at the sight. She came and stood next to him. All that gorgeous hair was secured in the back with one of those fancy rubber bands. Scrunchie. At least that's what Cynthie used to call them. He frowned, not wanting the specter of his ex intruding in this moment with Rory. Or at any time, frankly. She was his past.

Does this mean you're thinking of Rory in terms of your future? He frowned again at that thought, his mind going to yesterday's kiss.

"Sorry," Rory whispered. "I didn't mean to disturb your enjoyment of the sunrise."

"What?" He turned when she took a step back.

"I'll just—" she made a vague motion toward the house with her hand "I'll go back inside and—"

"Don't go." He pulled a hand from his pocket and reached for hers, his fingers curling around hers. They were cold and he urged her toward him, hoping to use his body heat to warm her.

"I thought maybe you wanted to be alone."

He shook his head. "It would be a shame to not share this."

"Thanks." She smiled and scooted over.

He wanted to pull her into his arms and really warm her—and himself—but he contented himself with holding this small part of her when he ached to hold all of her. Who knew such a chaste action could bring so much satisfaction? He leaned closer, drawn by the scent of orange blossoms.

Glowing red and filling the sky with brilliant color, the sun rose above the hill becoming visible through the trees. Rory sighed and he lightly squeezed her hand.

"Red sky in morning…"

"Sailors take warning," he finished and they both glanced at one another and grinned.

"But it was beautiful," she said.

"Stunning," he replied and met her dark-eyed gaze. "And I don't mean just the sunrise."

Her cheeks flushed pinker than normal. When was the last time he'd made a woman blush? He kinda liked the feeling it gave him. He'd lost more than the lower part of his leg with the amputation. It was as if the surgeon had taken more than damaged flesh and bone.

"Flatterer," she said, shaking her head at him, but she grinned. "How about some coffee? I was going to make some when I saw you from the kitchen window. I hope you don't mind I decided to join you."

"I'm glad you did."

"After yesterday, I was surprised you'd be up so early."

"I thought farm work started at dawn."

"We're not exactly a traditional farm. My business is very small-scale at the moment. Supplying restaurants with organic herbs and vegetables hardly requires me to rise at dawn. I spend much of my time weeding and harvesting small batches of herbs and vegetables and bringing them to restaurants."

"And yet you're up," he observed with a quirk to one eyebrow.

"Couldn't sleep. What's your excuse?"

"Same."

"Did your lack of sleep have anything to do with…"

"With what?"

"I don't want to pry."

"Go right ahead. You have my permission," he told her honestly.

"I noticed you snapped that rubber band several times yesterday. Was your leg bothering you?"

"Some," he admitted.

"Does that occur a lot?"

"I have good days and bad."

She glanced toward the house and back to him. "Would you like some breakfast? I don't offer as many selections as Aunt Polly's, but I do make a decent poached egg and toast."

He briefly thought about his vow to himself that he'd eat in the bunkhouse but eating alone as opposed to being with Rory in the warmth of that farmhouse kitchen was a no-brainer.

"Sure," he said and followed her into the house.

"Have a seat. I'll get some coffee. So, eggs and toast okay?"

"Sounds good."

She filled a mug with coffee and brought it to him. "That day when Phoebe was complaining about rules and you said you had a whole list of them, were you referring to things having to do with your…uh…residual limb?"

He saw her swallow around that last word and

reached for her hand. "It's okay to call it a stump. Cynthie couldn't even bring herself to say residual limb."

"I'm so sorry she hurt you, but I'm not sorry you kicked her to the curb."

He laughed. "Thanks, but she did most of the kicking."

This was the first time he could laugh when talking about his amputation. Was it the passage of time? Or Rory?

Maybe a combination of both, he told himself.

"Well, you're well rid of her if she couldn't accept you after what happened."

"She had this whole life planned out and when I lost my leg, she saw it slipping away."

"I still think she's the one who lost out, but I have to say I'm glad because you wouldn't be here otherwise."

"And you're glad I'm here?"

"Very."

"So am I."

A sudden cough broke the companionable silence that grew between the two of them. Walt interjected, "Maybe you two should put a tie or a sock around the door handle to warn a guy."

They both laughed.

"Or, you could babysit while I take Rory on a proper date," Mitch suggested. He was surprised at the ease with which the offer emerged, but once it was out there, he was pleased. No desire to take it back either.

Walt grumbled. "Breakfast at Polly's wasn't a proper date?"

"Not with the whole town watching."

"And just where to do you plan to take her where at least half the town won't be watching?"

Mitch laughed. "I hadn't thought that far ahead."

Walt scratched his chin. "I heard they have dancing now that the patio is open at Angelo's."

"And you're going to find someone to go with, so you'll be out of our way?"

"Smart a—aleck, I was suggesting you could take Rory."

"Dancing? I'm not sure I'm ready for that."

"Why wouldn't you— Oh. Damn, me and my big mouth. Sorry, son."

"It's okay. There's no reason I *can't* dance," Mitch said. "Wasn't there an old joke about a patient asking the doctor if he'd be able to play the violin after his injury…the doctor says yes, and the patient says great because I never could before."

Walt laughed and shook his head.

Mitch shrugged. "Maybe I should at least give it a try." He couldn't remember the last time he'd said that about something in his life but being around Rory and Phoebe was opening him up to possibilities he'd long considered dormant. Must be some of the little girl's princess magic, he figured.

"Even without dancing, I hear the patio is very romantic."

"And you're up on these things?" Mitch asked, feeling comfortable enough with Walt to tease him a bit. Walt grumbled something that sounded like wisenheimer. "Do you want to take her someplace romantic or not?"

"I do, but you know where that sort of stuff can lead."

"I'm not that old, kid. I know where this leads but I prefer not to consider that or I'd have to run you off."

"Ah, the quintessential farmer with the shotgun protecting his lovely daughter," Mitch said.

"Rory is an adult capable of making her own decisions."

"Guys, the capable adult is standing right here," Rory said, waving her hand.

"Sorry," Mitch and Walt mumbled at the same time.

"And what happens on or after this romantic date shall not be discussed," Mitch said. He liked and respected Walt but he didn't exactly want him privy to his private life and wanted to set some ground rules.

Walt grunted. "This very discussion will not be discussed."

And that was fine with Mitch. Despite having lived in close quarters while on deployment, he wasn't comfortable with Rory's family having intimate knowledge of their relationship.

After breakfast, Mitch and Walt went outside to assemble the heavy-duty greenhouse kit they'd ordered, leaving Rory in the house to make some business calls. The basic assembly taking less time than they expected, they stood back to admire their work.

Walt removed his cap and wiped his forehead with his arm. "I'll let you put the finishing touches on it."

"Sure."

"I'm going to take the tractor and mow the grass out around those apple trees," Walt told him.

"I can do that," Mitch said, wanting to not only pull his weight around the farm but to help Walt.

"I prefer doing myself."

Mitch frowned. Did he not trust him? He opened his mouth to protest, but Walt winked, patting the pocket on his chambray work shirt.

"I don't think you're fooling her," Mitch told him, hitching his chin at the cigar shaped lump.

"It's a game we play. If I have to sneak then I don't smoke as much," Walt said and disappeared.

Glancing at the house, Mitch saw why Walt left in such a hurry. Rory was making her way across the yard to the greenhouse.

"Where was Walt off to in such a hurry?" she asked as she approached.

"Said something about mowing around the apple trees."

"And smoking a cigar while doing it." She shook her head.

Mitch wiped a hand across his mouth, hoping to hide the smile that popped up. It wasn't his place to rat out the old guy. "What do you think?"

He made a sweeping motion with his arm toward the interior of the greenhouse.

"Oh, wow, this is awesome," Rory said as they walked inside the completed structure. "You did an awesome job."

"Walt helped too," he pointed out.

"True, but you've been the impetus to get all this done." She turned to him and smiled. "And so quickly too."

"Hmm, does that mean I'm working myself out of a job?" He'd hate to think so because he was enjoying being here more than he'd ever expected. Not just in Loon Lake but on this farm. He could tell himself it was because he'd been reunited with Sarge but he'd be deceiving himself by thinking that was the only reason. All he had to do was look at the smile on Rory's face to know it for the lie it was.

"You might eventually want something bigger but we wanted to get this one together first before ordering multiples," Mitch told her.

"Thanks so much," she turned to him and standing on her toes, she threw her arms around him in a hug.

"It was my pleasure." And he'd be sure to do more if that's the thanks he got.

He met her gaze and his arms went around her and their lips met in a kiss. A tractor started up behind the barn and she hastily pulled away.

"I…um…" She made a motion with her hand.

He cleared his throat. "Do you know what plants you're going to put in here?"

She glanced around. "I know I want to try lavender again and I'm thinking I might like to plant some ube."

"What's ube?" he asked, not sure he'd ever heard of it.

"Purple yams. I'd like to try making some jam. Tavie already agreed to carry some at the General Store if I made it."

"Purple yam jam?"

She laughed and sent a tingle down his spine. He loved her laugh.

"So, they're like sweet potatoes?" he asked.

"Actually, yams are different. Sweet potatoes grow in the ground like regular potatoes, beets, carrots, stuff like that. Yams, on the other hand, are vines," she said her tone enthusiastic and her eyes sparkling.

He found himself hanging on her every word despite not having any previous interest in yams or sweet potatoes and never having even heard of ube.

She suddenly frowned. "Of course I might fail. Even with putting them in a greenhouse. They're originally from the Philippines so a totally different environment."

"Well, if anyone can grow them in Vermont, I'm sure it will be you," he told her, wanting to see that smile again and bring back the sparkle to her eyes.

"Thank you."

She bestowed that smile on him again. "If everything is ready, I'm going to go and get some of the plants I bought in anticipation of this being finished."

"The ones I saw lined up by the barn?" he asked and when she nodded, he continued, "I got you one of those flatbed carts they use at the garden center."

"You did? How did you manage that?"

"You just have to run quicker than they do," he said, tongue firmly in cheek.

"What? No! You—"

"Joking." Chuckling, he held up his hands. "Turns out the owner's son is Airborne and we chatted."

Although he'd only been in Loon Lake a short time, the place was wearing off on him. Or maybe he was finally finding another place where he fit in as he had done in the army. After his career ended, he'd wondered if he'd ever fit in like that again.

Her brows drawn together; she gave him a speculative look. "And she just gave you one?"

"It's one she was going to replace so it's old and a bit rickety but it's good enough for your purposes," he said and that was close enough to the truth. He'd planned to buy Rory a new one but knew she would insist on paying him back so he'd made a deal to buy the used one from the garden center. Most of it was the absolute truth, including the son who was an Airborne Ranger. "You won't have to make so many trips back and forth with bags of fertilizer or soil."

"Thank you for doing this and for even thinking of it." She stood on her tiptoes and kissed his cheek, smiling as she pulled away.

It was a chaste and circumspect kiss but it kick-started his blood flowing.

"Would you like to go to Angelo's on Saturday?" he heard himself asking under the glow of that smile.

"Angelo's?"

"I heard the patio was uh…nice," he felt heat creep into his cheeks.

"So did I since I was standing in the same kitchen when you and Walt were discussing it."

He rubbed his chin as if trying to remember. "So that *was* you. I was trying to remember."

She poked his upper arm. "Wisenheimer," she muttered imitating Walt.

They both laughed. He enjoyed these light moments with her. "Do you think that was Walt's way of giving us his blessing?"

"At the very least, I would say it means he trusts you."

He chuckled. "That's because he can't see what's inside my head when I look at you."

"Oh, Walt's not so old that he's forgotten those feelings," she said with a smirk.

"He never married?" he asked.

"No, and it's too bad because under that marine sergeant exterior he's really a sweet guy. He deserves a good woman."

Mitch laughed. "Maybe I should introduce him to my mother. They're about the same age and she's been alone for a long time. It would be nice to see her find someone to share her life with."

"You're free to invite her for a visit."

"Maybe I will," he said but he was thinking about introducing his mother to Rory and Phoebe.

That was a big step. Was he ready to take it? His mom had been disappointed when he and Cynthie had split. He knew his mom had hoped to see him settled. Although she didn't overstep, he knew she'd like some grandchildren someday. While she was young enough to enjoy them, she'd said. Yeah, no pressure there.

No, that wasn't entirely fair. His mother had never pressured him directly about grandchildren. She'd stressed that she just wanted to see him happy as any mother would. Of course he wanted that too. Could he find that here?

"Can we start bringing the plants in here? I don't want to get in your way if you're not finished yet."

Rory's question brought him out of his head. "I'm finished but you haven't answered my question yet."

"I didn't? My mistake because I'd love nothing better to go to Angelo's with you," she said, her cheeks filled with color.

"Great."

"Just the two of us?" she asked, her smile a bit tentative.

"Unchaperoned? Hmm…let me think…"

She laughed. "That would mean closing the place to the rest of the Loon Lake because everyone will be watching us."

"But we'll have our own table, right?"

She nodded. "Absolutely."

"So, that's okay with you?" he asked. He wanted to be sure they were on the same wavelength about what was brewing between them. He had nothing against Phoebe joining them for certain things but this romantic patio sounded like an adults only date.

"Absolutely. If Saturday is good for you, Phoebe will be with her dad so…"

"So, it's a date and I mean that in every sense this time."

"And unchaperoned," she said.

Her smile glowed and he was pretty sure if they opened him up right now his insides would be glowing too.

"Did you have plants you wanted to bring in here?" he asked.

If they didn't start working he might end up kissing her again and the last thing he wanted was for Walt to catch them kissing again.

"Yeah, I guess we should be doing that, huh? Walt will be wondering what mischief we were getting up to." she said.

"My thoughts exactly," he said, already looking forward to Saturday.

The next afternoon Mitch was in the barn stacking the bags of chicken pellets he'd picked up from the feed store that morning. Now that the chicken coop and exterior area were completed, Rory was eager to add the chickens.

"Mr. Mitch. Mr. Mitch," Phoebe called breathlessly as she came running into the barn. "Look what I got for you."

She proudly held up a hot-pink silicone wristband.

"For me?"

"Uh-huh. It's so much prettier than the one you have."

"The one I...?" He glanced at the rubber band on his wrist. "Well, I certainly appreciate the gesture, but I—"

"Mommy let me pick it out all by myself. I used some of my birthday money," she told him, pride in her voice. "Mommy said she'd pay but I wanted to use my own money so it would be special from me."

How was he supposed to refuse it now? He wouldn't hurt her feelings for anything. "You're sure you wouldn't rather wear it?"

"I gots one too." She held up her arm and twisted it back and forth. "See."

"Yes, I see that. Now we'll match." He could barely get the words out past the sudden closing of his throat. The fact this precious child cared for him enough to pick out a gift and want to use her own money brought on an alarming rush of feelings. He struggled to get them under control.

"Yeah, Mommy said maybe I should get a different color but I wanted to match," she was telling him.

"I'll wear it proudly," Mitch told her as he slipped the wristband over his hand.

"Aren't you gonna take off the ugly one?" Phoebe asked with a scowl.

"Phoebe! Remember your manners," Rory admonished her daughter as she entered the barn.

"I gotta be polite. Mommy says it's a rule unless they touch me and I don't want to be touched." Phoebe said.

"Both sound like good rules," he told her and removed the rubber band. Backing up Rory in her parenting seemed important. And if anyone did any harm to this precious child they'd have to answer to him, the thought fiercely.

"Is you okay, Mr. Mitch?" Phoebe was peering up at him.

He smoothed out his face and smiled. "Yes, and I'll wear your gift proudly."

Of course he wasn't a parent to Phoebe, nothing close, but he had the urge to be a good role model as well as a protector of her innocence. He also knew in that moment he'd do anything to protect her which included sparing her feelings. Nothing could make him remove her gift. Rory joined them and stood next to him, close enough for her scent to tickle his senses, close enough to feel the natural warmth from her body. Or was it because he was supersensitive to everything about this woman?

"See, Mommy, he likes it. I was right, wasn't I?" Phoebe gazed up at her mother for confirmation.

Rory reached down and gave her daughter a hug. "Of course you were."

Sarge appeared at the entrance to the barn and Phoebe ran over to him.

Rory leaned toward Mitch. "You don't have to wear that. You can pretend you lost it."

Mitch shook his head. "And hurt her feelings? No way. I think I'm secure enough in my manhood to wear it."

And he found he meant it. He'd wear a hot-pink wristband day and night rather than disappoint this little girl.

"Thank you," she said.

"There's no need to thank me," he told her.

He was grateful Phoebe cared enough for him to pick out such a caring gift.

Was Phoebe's thoughtfulness at picking out this special gift mean she was choosing him too? He rubbed the sudden piercing sensation near his heart.

Chapter Twelve

"Does you live in a nice big house with lots of rooms, Mr. Mitch?" Phoebe asked.

Two days after making a date with Rory Mitch was working in the barn. He grunted as he hefted the bag onto the pile and reached for another. Fifty pounds of garden soil wasn't so bad to handle. "You know I'm staying at the bunkhouse."

He glanced toward the entrance to the barn. Where was Rory? Why was Phoebe here in the barn by herself? He didn't mind her curiosity, he found it endearing but he had work to do and he didn't want her to get hurt. Doing his job while looking out for her safety was not a compatible combination.

"Where's your mom?" he asked. He needed to get these bags ready to go into the greenhouse. Maybe he should take her back to the house. "I thought your mom said you were going with your dad today?"

"Mommy's waiting for him to come."

Why would she send Phoebe out here? Did Rory have something to talk with her ex about that she didn't want Phoebe to hear? He blew out his breath and dug deep for patience. Rory could have at least warned him she was sending Phoebe to the barn.

"I meant your other house. The one you had before you came to visit us. Mommy said you lived in someplace called North Caroline. Is it really big?" Phoebe asked again.

"No," he said and swiped at the sweat on his forehead with his arm. Why was she so fixated on his living quarters?

"Oh."

It was one word. Just one. But spoken with such emotion he paused instead of picking up the next bag.

Phoebe was looking up at him, her lower lip quivering. The skin at his nape itched. As much as he liked Phoebe, he sometimes felt as though he were picking his way through a minefield when he spoke with her. And why did he care so much? He knew already he'd do anything for her. Was he having second thoughts about getting in deeper with these people? "I have an apartment."

He left out the part about it being only two rooms furnished with items that looked as though they were purchased from a cheap motel liquidation sale. Sorta like the Stargazer Inn and now the bunkhouse. After spending so much time in temporary places while on deployment, his needs were basic, but he did sometimes wonder what a real, permanent residence would be like. Someplace like Bowie Griffin's farm. Was he destined to live in other people's places?

Phoebe continued to look up at him with that lower lip stuck out. She studied him with an unnerving intensity. "But it's real pretty, huh, Mr. Mitch?"

He gnawed the inside of his cheek under her scrutiny. The little girl who loved bright colors and shiny baubles would hate his place. Too drab for a kid like her. Hell, he even found it depressing at times. He hated to think why he thought it was okay. Those army docs would have a field day analyzing that.

Phoebe was still staring at him, so he shrugged. "It's adequate for my needs."

She scowled. "I don't know what that means."

Yeah, me neither, kid. Most of his places had been nothing more than shelter. Period. He scratched the back of his neck. What started as a simple conversation was suddenly fraught with pitfalls. What did this pint-sized dynamo want from him? He suspected she had a purpose behind her questions. "Well... I—"

"Phoebe Jane Walsh! I have been looking everywhere for you."

His savior marched into the barn, and he could've kissed her. But then everything lately seemed to end in thoughts of him kissing Rory. Or with him actually kissing her. Best not to think about that now, he cautioned himself.

"But, Mommy, I been here the whole time. Right, Mr. Mitch?"

"Well, I had no idea where you'd disappeared to." Rory cupped her palm over her daughter's head. "You shouldn't be bothering him while he's trying to work, isn't that right, Mr. Mitch?"

"Was I bothering you?" Phoebe looked up at him, her lower lip wobbling once again.

He gulped. Facing a band of insurgents armed with Kalashnikovs was preferable to these two staring expectantly at him...

"She wasn't bothering me," he finally said. What else could he do? "She was just asking about my living arrangements."

Phoebe put her hands on her hips and confronted him. "You say lots of stuff I don't understand."

"I apologize, Miss Phoebe. You're very smart and I guess I assumed you understand almost everything."

She nodded. "That's okay. I like it when you tell me stuff even if I don't understand all of it."

"I'm glad." And that was the truth. For someone who hadn't spent a lot of time around children, he was finding he enjoyed his time with Phoebe. Even following her meandering conversations, while sometimes challenging, was for the most part enjoyable.

"Why were you asking him about where he lives?" Rory asked.

"For when Uncle Bo kicks us out. Where would we go? What would we do if we don't have no place to live, Mommy?"

Mitch's pulse picked up. Was her brother threatening to kick them out? From everything he'd sensed when either Rory or Walt mentioned Bowie, they revered him as some sort of hero. Why would he kick out his sister and niece?

"What?" Rory asked, her tone incredulous. "What are you talking about? Uncle Bo isn't going to kick us out. This is our home too. At least for a while."

Did she have plans to move out at some point? Mitch wondered. She seemed to be settling in. And he'd been under the impression he was helping her do that. Of course he didn't mind helping a fellow soldier, or in this case sailor, but it wasn't the same as helping Rory and Phoebe.

"But he said so, Mommy," Phoebe was insisting.

"When did Bo say something like that?"

"When you asked him what would happen when he gets tired from saving the world and wants to come back here to live and he said he would kick us out."

"Oh, sweetie, he was teasing." Rory squatted in front of Phoebe. "We were talking about when he *retires* from the military, and I asked what he'd do if we were still living here. You know how Uncle Bo likes to tease you about stuff. That's what he was doing with me."

Relief swept through Mitch at the simple explanation. Although he didn't have siblings, he could imagine a big brother teasing his sister like that. Even if they were adults. They say you don't miss what you don't have but at that moment he wondered how it would have felt having a close relationship like that. Yes, he was close to his mom but she was just one person. Rory, Phoebe, Walt, the missing Bowie seemed to have a strong family bond.

Phoebe scrunched up her face. "But you're all growed up. Can he do that?"

"Grownups tease other grownups all the time. Especially when they're siblings."

"What does that mean?"

"Siblings? It means Bo and I are brother and sister. That's why he was teasing me. He wouldn't really kick us out of our home."

Mitch rubbed his chest. So she did think of the farm as home. He was glad to be helping her get her business up and running.

"How come we don't have a place of our own? Maybe we should move back in with Daddy."

Mitch stiffened at Phoebe's suggestion. It shouldn't matter to him how Rory felt about her ex. It wasn't like he was sticking around Loon Lake forever. Right?

"I've explained before that won't be happening, sweetie. Daddy and I will always be your parents even if we don't live together."

"What if Uncle Bo gets a family and there isn't enough room for us?" Phoebe reasoned.

"I don't think that's going to happen anytime soon, but we'll be getting a place of our own someday."

"And no one will be able to kick us out?"

"Maybe once we get a place of our own, Mr. Mitch can come to live with us," Phoebe suggested.

"What? Why would you say that?" Rory asked.

Yeah, why would you say that? Not that he found himself as reluctant at the prospect of shacking up with the Walsh women once again as he might have imagined...

"Because it sounds like his place is kinda yucky."

Mitch choked on a suppressed laugh.

"Oh my God, Mitch, I'm so sorry. Phoebe, why would you say something like that? That's rude."

"But he called it *ad-quit*. I don't know what that means but it doesn't sound very nice."

"The kid's right. I didn't make it sound very appealing," he admitted, barely keeping his lips from curving upward in a smile.

"Well, you should still apologize," Rory insisted.

The little girl sniffed. "I'm sorry if I hurt your feelings, Mr. Mitch."

He might regret the gesture when it came time to stand, but he hunkered down in front of her. "It's okay. I know you didn't mean to hurt my feelings."

Phoebe threw her arms around him, and he hugged her back. And it felt right. More right than anything had in the past year.

"Mary, I can't thank you enough for helping me with all this paperwork," Rory told her friend later that day after Curt had picked up Phoebe.

Rory was with Mary Wilson in the small office she made for herself in the barn.

In addition to running a successful non-profit that provided summer camp experiences for children in foster care and other disadvantaged children, Mary was a CPA.

She'd agreed to look over Rory's paperwork and help her get billing software up and running. Rory was determined to get the business end running smoothly for her farm to table business.

"You're welcome. I'm grateful you've agreed to adopt most of my chickens. I'm glad they'll be going to a good home. That set up you have is fantastic," the other woman told her.

"Well, that is all thanks to Mitch," Rory said.

"The new farm hand I'm hearing so much about?" Mary grinned and brushed a dark curl from her cheek, tucking it behind her ear.

"News travels fast around here," Rory said, silently cursing her pale skin which was probably the color of the silicone bracelet Phoebe gave Mitch.

"I heard you and the little one had breakfast with him. Do you have breakfast with all your employees or just the super sexy ones?"

"Oh, so you've seen Mitch?"

"No, but you've just confirmed what I've heard." Mary laughed. "Do I detect some interest there?"

Rory heaved a sigh. Why try to deny it? Everyone in town was enjoying speculating no matter what she said. And once they showed up together at Angelo's the town would view them as a couple. "I'd be lying if I said no."

"Excuse the interruption, ladies, but Walt is back with the lumber you wanted. Where do you want me to stack it?"

Rory startled at the sound of Mitch's voice in the doorway to the office. How much had he heard? Did he hear them refer to him as sexy? Her cheeks had probably passed hot-pink by now and were in the crimson levels.

"Lumber?" Rory asked, trying to remember why she'd wanted it.

"Um, well, I really should be leaving," Mary said.

"Where are my manners?" Rory asked, trying to recover. "Mary, this is Mitch Sawicki. He's... um, new in town."

Mary stuck her hand out. "It's a pleasure to finally meet you. You'll have to forgive us, we're a friendly little town but newcomers are a bit of a novelty. I know because I was a flatlander—that's a newcomer—once myself."

"It's a pleasure to meet you," Mitch shook her hand and smiled.

Rory noticed that Mary might be married but she obviously wasn't immune to that crooked smile, if the color on her cheeks was any indication. And she wasn't jealous if that smile was bestowed on someone else. Nope. Besides, Mary was happily married to her soul mate.

"Right, Rory?" Mary said.

"What? I'm sorry... I was..." Too busy being jealous.

Mary appeared to be smothering a grin and Rory sent her a look full of mock disapproval which Mary returned with a sweet smile and a twinkle in her eyes.

"I was saying that you have a good grasp of the

new software, so I'll be taking off," Mary said and turned to Mitch. "It was a pleasure meeting you but I'm afraid I left Brody home alone with the kids."

"He's excellent with them," Rory said.

A lot like Mitch is with Phoebe, she thought, her gaze seeking him out.

Mary nodded, a dreamy expression washing over her face that Rory assumed was caused by Mary's thoughts of Brody.

"He is," Mary said. "But now that Alice has started walking she's an absolute terror with Elliott and his things. She's like an avenging Godzilla with his carefully constructed Playmobil adventure sets. So, call me when you're ready to come get the chickens."

"I will. We're just about ready. I want to be sure they're absolutely safe from predators."

"I told Brody I wouldn't let go of those chickens unless it was to someone like Rory who will take good care of them," Mary said to Mitch as she passed him on her way out of the barn.

Mitch came to stand next to Rory as she watched Mary leave. "She the one who runs the summer camps with her husband?"

Rory nodded. "Yes. Believe it or not, Brody was like some hermit living out on his farm until Mary and Elliott exploded into his life. He's like a changed man since he married Mary and adopted Elliott."

He grinned at her.

"What?" she asked and touched her face to see if she had something stuck on it.

He touched his forefinger to the end of her nose. "I think you like fairy tales as much as your daughter."

"Is that so bad?" Was he teasing her or criticizing? She held her breath, waiting to see what he would say.

"I think it's exactly what this world needs."

She exhaled and smiled, lifting her face toward his and wishing he'd kiss her. Again. She quite liked his kisses. Now that she knew how heavenly those lips felt against hers, she wanted more. Much, much more.

But she had responsibilities. With an impressionable daughter she needed to put first, she wasn't a summer fling type person. Has she ever been?

He must've seen something in her expression because he pulled away. She tried not to let it bother her. After all, he'd asked her on a date. Unless he was suddenly regretting— No, she scolded herself. Don't start imagining scenarios and spoil things.

"So, what was the lumber for? I thought we were finished with the construction portion of the chicken coop," he said.

"We are. I'm setting up a booth for my farm-to-table business. People will be showcasing local crafts and businesses on the town green at the annual Independence Day picnic. I wanted to have a few things plus I've ordered some pamphlets. What do you think of pick your own strawberries?"

"I'm not sure I have an opinion." He frowned. "Should I? Where would we be picking these strawberries?"

She laughed and shook her head. "I'm just thinking out loud about future ventures."

"Look, I know you told Phoebe that your brother was joking about kicking you out…"

"When he bought this place, he said he had plans on being a gentlemen farmer. Last time he was here he accused me of turning this into a profitable business," she said and laughed.

He touched her arm. "Then maybe—"

"He gave me free reign as long as I continued to take care of it while he sits on the porch with his feet up, sipping whiskey and watching me do all the work." She laid her hand over his and laughed. "Of course the jokes on me because he'd probably do it."

His gaze dropped and she followed it to where her hand rested over his. She hastily dropped her hand, but he picked it back up and kissed the tips of her fingers.

"I thought I heard an old pickup. I'm only willing to get caught kissing you so many times," he said and gently let go of her hand. "Now, what can I do to help with this booth of yours?"

"I know you didn't sign up for this construction when you agreed to the job."

He raised an eyebrow. "Agreed to the job? The way I recall it, I insisted you give me the job."

She expelled her breath in a chuckle. "You sorta did."

"So that's settled. Tell me what you need," he said.

"I need some display tables for my goods. I had hoped to borrow some from the church, but other people beat me to it."

"Do you want me to see about buying or renting some?" he asked.

"Thanks, but that's what the lumber is for. I just haven't had time to assemble them," she said.

"Do I look like IKEA?"

"Well…"

"C'mon," he grumbled but his twitching lips gave him away. "Lead the way, boss."

She was enjoying seeing the playful side to Mitch. Oh, who was she kidding? She enjoyed seeing all the facets of his personality emerging. Her feelings for him were deepening day by day. Not only was it scary but exhilarating as well.

Mitch spent the next morning working with Walt as they figured out a way to partially assemble a booth and table for her display. As he had explained to her, they would need to transport everything to the town green so it needed to be sturdy but also portable. From the way she blushed, he knew she hadn't given that a thought.

Luckily, Walt had anticipated that very thing and had purchased a collection of hinges to make the legs and other parts of the display collapsible.

"Walt?" Rory asked from the entrance to the barn. "May I borrow your truck? Mary called and asked if I could pick up the chickens today. Some-one loaned her a bunch of cages to transport them and I want to take advantage of that plus the fact Phoebe is with Curt's parents today."

"Sure." Walt dug in the pocket of his overalls

for his keys. "Do you need help? We're about done here."

Mitch stepped forward, anticipating some alone time with Rory, even if it was only in the truck transporting chickens. "I don't mind helping."

Walt made a noise and Mitch glanced at him.

"Take Mitch. Chasing chickens around isn't my idea of a way to spend an afternoon," the other man said, grinning broadly at Mitch.

Either chasing chickens was something Mitch was going to regret or Walt knew why he'd volunteered.

Walt tossed Mitch the keys. "Have fun rounding up hens."

Mitch ended up driving the old pickup with Rory acting as navigator.

"This is a nice drive over here," he said as they turned off the state highway onto a county road. The narrow road wound past rolling pastures broken up by fences or forested sections. Exactly the kind of scenery Mitch had expected to find in Vermont.

"Those are sugar maples," Rory said as they passed a dense stand of trees.

"The kind they get maple syrup from?" He knew the real deal was made from boiling down the sap from maple trees, hence the name, but he hadn't really thought about the process.

"Yeah, they'll tap the trees to collect the sap in February and March."

Mitch shot her a brief glance. "Don't tell me you have plans."

She hooted a laugh. "It takes at least forty years for a tree to grow big enough to tap. But if you take care of your trees, you can tap them indefinitely. Some of the ones they're tapping now, were saplings during the Civil War."

He looked at the stand of trees they were passing with renewed respect. "So you're not willing to wait around for forty years to try it?"

"I have to wait until next year for the strawberry plants I'm planting now to bear fruit and that feels like forever. So no, I'm not going into the maple syrup business."

"Unless you bought forty-year-old trees," he said.

She groaned. "Don't give me any ideas. I come up with enough by myself."

He laughed, thoroughly enjoying his time with Rory. Yes, he was physically attracted to her, and hoping at some point to take it to the next level, but he also liked her, like talking to her, teasing her.

"There's the turn off," she said and pointed to a narrow dirt road. There was a red wooden sign with white letters proclaiming 'Camp Life Launch' at the entrance.

He took the turnoff, a little sorry their time alone was coming to an end.

"That's the Wilson's place up ahead," she said after a few minutes and pointed.

A white two-story farmhouse with a red metal roof sat on a large tract of flat land. A covered porch ran across the front and wrapped around one side and a large red barn sat off to the side and behind the home.

He pulled up to a parking area near the barn and stopped the truck next to an official looking red SUV.

"Huh. Cal Pope must be here," Rory said as the truck shut down with a bit of back talk from the old engine. "Looks like his vehicle. He's the Fire Marshal."

As Rory spoke, Mary emerged from the barn followed by two men, one dressed in blue jeans and a chambray shirt and one wearing navy-blue pants and matching shirt with a fire department logo.

Mitch jumped out of the old pickup and went around the front to help Rory out of the passenger side.

"Thanks," she said when he offered her a hand.

"Good to see you again," Mary said to Mitch and introduced Mitch to her husband Brody and family friend Cal Pope. After the introductions, Mary smiled at Rory. "Are we ready to round up some hens?"

"You know how much I'd love to help, but I'm headed over to Julian Bond's to see if I can repair his fence. He claims the damage is our fault. I stopped to see if I could tempt Brody to come along and help," Cal said.

"And he knows I owe him a favor," Brody said.

"What happened? If you don't mind my asking." Mitch's curiosity was aroused and found to his surprise he didn't want to be left out. When had becoming part of the close-knit Loon Lake community become part of the mission?

"A deer got her head stuck in between the bars of Julian's fancy fence and someone saw it and called the fire department. They freed the doe, but the rookie got a bit carried away with the jaws of life. I'm going to see if I can make it look presentable." Cal rubbed his chin as he studied Mitch. "How about you? You interested in coming along with us? We could always use another hand."

"It's sounds better than corralling hens," Brody said.

Cal laughed. "Gathering hens sounds a lot like herding cats."

"It is." Brody nodded his head and gave Mitch a raised eyebrows look.

"Why does the name Julian Bond sound familiar?" Mitch asked. A thought hit him, "Is he the Speedo guy?"

Brody belted out a laugh and clapped Mitch on the shoulder. "Sounds like you're one of us already."

"You guys go and do manly things. Rory and I can handle this," Mary said and turned to Rory as if for confirmation.

Rory looked to Mitch, and he shrugged. He probably should be embarrassed by how much being included meant to him but he wasn't. He hadn't realized how much he missed being a part of something, a part of a community.

But it wasn't just any community he wanted to

be a part of. It was this one, here with these people. With Rory, Phoebe, and Walt.

"You can deduct if from my pay," he told Rory with a wink.

"I'll bill the Loon Lake Fire Department," Rory said with a grin.

Cal rubbed his hands together. "We'd better shove off before these ladies change their minds."

Brody went to Mary and gave her a quick kiss before heading to Cal's SUV.

Mitch had the urge to do the same with Rory but curbed it at the last minute. He didn't have that right and wasn't sure how she'd feel about that in front of her friends.

And he wasn't sure how *he'd* feel about it. Was he ready for that? Like his conversations with Phoebe, dealing with his conflicting emotions was like picking his way through a minefield.

The next morning Rory stood at the hen enclosure, watching her new chickens peck their way around the yard. She'd been so excited she'd risen early and gone to let her girls out into the fenced-in area of their new home.

She had Mitch to thank for this. Yes, Walt had helped but Mitch had done his research and made sure her hens were not only comfortable but protected from dangerous predators.

Sarge whined and sat beside her; his attention riveted on the chickens as they learned their new surroundings.

"I hope you don't see them as potential dinner," she told the dog and rubbed his ear.

He gave an excited yip.

"Was that a yes or—" She stopped and turned when the dog loped off with a happy bark.

Mitch was making his way across the yard. He bent down and greeted Sarge, who was showering him with affection.

Mitch pulled a rubber toy from his pocket and gave it a toss.

As she watched him, her heart gave a special *ker-thump* that seemed to be reserved just for him.

He'd only been here a short time but she couldn't picture the place without him. But she would have to at some point. She couldn't imagine him being content to be a poorly paid farm hand for the rest of his life.

"I can't thank you enough for bringing this dream alive for me," she told him as he came to stand beside her.

He shrugged. "Walt helped."

"I know but…"

"And you had the vision, I just did the grunt work."

"You know," she said and turned to him with a giant smile. "You're right. I'm going to take all the credit."

"As long as I don't go into town and hear about how you fixed Julian Bond's fence," he said, winging the toy out into the unknown, confident Sarge would find and retrieve it.

"I heard that was all down to Cal and Brody. Not

sure anyone else was with them." She bumped her shoulder against his, enjoying the playful moment. "Would you like to come in for some coffee? I was on my way back inside to fix breakfast."

"An offer I can't refuse," he said and fell into step beside her as they made their way back into the house. "Where's Phoebe?"

"She was still sleeping. I'm sure she'll be up soon."

"I heard the guys talking about some parking lot carnival in town," he said as he held the wooden screen door to the kitchen open for her to enter ahead of him.

"Yeah, it's a yearly tradition sponsored by the Parks and Recreation Department to raise money," she said, thinking about past ones. "The event has just as much for kids as adults."

There were kiddie rides plus lots of arts and craft vendors selling their wares and bake sales to raise money for church groups and youth activities.

"Would you like to come with us?" she asked.

"I'd be honored. Thanks for including me."

"My pleasure," she said.

Curt had always complained that the carnival was tacky but she actually loved it. Something about the lights, sounds, and smells that intrigued her.

Sharing the experience with Mitch would only enhance her enjoyment.

The early portion of the evening was dedicated to letting Phoebe lead them around to the various kiddie rides and booths set up for children.

Rory couldn't help but notice all the looks they were getting from everyone. They were certainly giving the gossips a lot of fodder by walking around looking like a family.

"You realize I'll never remember all these people's names," Mitch leaned over to whisper to her after being introduced yet again to someone who stopped to greet them.

"You don't have to," she said, patting his arm. "They'll remember yours."

He hooted a laugh, causing several people to look in his direction. "Should I be concerned?"

"Mr. Mitch, I want to go on that one," Phoebe said before Rory could answer his question.

Phoebe pointed at a kiddie coaster shaped like a train with a smiling engine on the front.

Mitch turned to her and raised an eyebrow in invitation but Rory shook her head.

"I thought you said you enjoyed the carnival," he said with a frown.

"I do but I don't have to ride all the rides to get enjoyment from it."

"If you say so."

Rory was pleased by what a good sport Mitch was being by riding the things that she refused to. He and her daughter would laugh and call her a wimp but she was adamant that some of the motions made her ill. She wanted to enjoy the entire evening without being plagued by dizziness or nausea.

Curt had agreed to meet them there so he and his parents could enjoy part of the evening with

Phoebe. She knew he was only doing it for his parents but she wasn't going to spoil Phoebe's evening with a petty reminder that he considered the whole event tacky.

Later that evening after the child hand off had been dealt with, Mitch slipped her hand into his as they walked around the midway.

"I haven't been to one of these since I was a kid," Mitch said.

"I'm glad you're enjoying it," she said. "You are having fun, aren't you?"

"Absolutely," he said. "I don't suppose I can tempt you on any of the adult rides?"

She winced. "I…"

"What is it you like if you don't do all the rides?"

"Atmosphere?"

"You telling me or asking me?"

She shrugged. "It reminds of happy memories from my childhood."

"Then I'm glad I came you are sharing it with me." He squeezed her hand and the pad of his thumb moved in lazy circles around her palm.

She wanted to respond to his comment, but she couldn't because she was too busy trying to breathe—it was obvious her lungs were directly attached to her palm because they refused to work while his thumb caressed her. But it wasn't simply his thumb, it was the whole package. He anticipated where she only guessed at what she needed. And he was happy to do anything she asked without an ulterior motive. And when he smiled at Phoebe… or her…she was dead in the water.

He must be falling for Rory Walsh because his
stomach was tied in knots. He hadn't felt this way
about a woman in ages. Had he ever felt like this?
He'd fallen for Cynthie but this felt different. What
he was feeling for Rory was more than lust, more
than thinking it was time to settle down.

"C'mon, it'll be fun to try out some of those
games of chance."

"Chance?" He raised an eyebrow. "It's my understanding that they're all rigged."

"But it's still fun to try."

"But I don't wanna!" he said in a jokingly whiny
voice.

"You sound like my daughter."

"And that's a good thing, right?" He laughed.

"If you want to be likened to a four-year-old who
wears tinfoil crowns and red boots."

"Tell me she doesn't she wear those things to
bed?"

"She wanted to the first night she had them."

"Did you let her?" He had a feeling that she had.
He suspected that Rory, for all her rules, was indulgent in certain things. If wearing her new boots
was important to Phoebe, Rory would have a hard
time saying no. He knew he would.

"Yes, but after she fell asleep, I sneaked in and
took them off. Her feet had already started to
sweat."

"You're a good mom."

"I…" she stopped and gave him a searching

stare. "Thank you. I worry how much the divorce has affected her."

"From what I've seen, you're good at setting rules and boundaries but not so stiff that you wouldn't allow her to wear those boots to bed."

"After the first night, we compromised with her bringing them to bed instead of wearing them."

"I'll bet she's a good negotiator."

Rory laughed. "Or I'm a pushover."

"I wouldn't say that."

He leaned toward her and brushed his mouth against hers, uncaring if the whole town saw him. He was staking his claim. She'd said there was no way she was ever getting back with her ex and she'd made it clear that she was attracted to him, so he was free to move in. And he intended to before someone else in this town realized what a wonderful woman was living amongst their midst.

"You weren't by any chance a sharpshooter or anything?"

"Sharpshooter?" he grinned. "You mean a sniper? The answer is no. Why?"

She pointed with her chin at the carnival's shooting booth. "No one has ever won me anything."

"Never?"

"Nope."

"What about all those high school boys that you probably came here with? You said you've been coming to this thing ever since you could remember." He glanced around at all the teens roaming around the midway. "This looks like the place to hang out."

"It was, but I didn't date much in high school."

"I find that hard to believe."

"Believe it. It wasn't easy being the girl whose parents had been killed in that notorious accident."

He put his arm around her shoulder and pulled her close. "I'm sorry you had to go through that."

She put her arms around his waist and squeezed. "Thanks. Now go and win me a bear."

"I told you these things were rigged," Mitch grumbled. He hadn't been too bad a shot in the army, but that didn't mean he'd be a good one at a carnival game.

"Making excuses, Sawicki?"

"Challenge accepted," he said and slapped a bill onto the wooden counter. He picked up one of the air guns and tested the scope, then took an experimental shot and missed.

She raised an eyebrow at him.

"That was a test shot. Show me which prize you want."

She looked at the colorful but inexpensive stuffed animals hanging around the three sides of the booth. Her gaze stopped at a stuffed horned owl and she pointed. Mitch's gaze followed her pointing finger.

"Stand back and prepare to be amazed," he said. It wasn't until he'd said it that he realized that was something the old Mitch would have said. The one who'd been brimming with confidence. The one he thought he'd lost along with the lower half of his left leg.

He took several more test shots to get the feel of the gun and to see how accurate—make that inaccurate—the sight was.

"I thought you said you were good at this," Rory complained but grinned wickedly when he scowled at her.

"I'm getting the feel of the gun," he told her and leaned down and kissed the end of her nose.

She blushed and glanced around.

Damn. Was she embarrassed to have people see them together as a couple? Was she—

She interrupted his negative thoughts by tugging on his shirt. Bringing his face closer, she stood on her toes and gave him a kiss on the lips.

"Win me something, soldier," she said and pulled away.

"Yes, ma'am."

He took careful aim, keeping the gun's eccentricities in mind, and pulled the trigger. Not stopping after that first satisfying ping, he continued until he'd won enough for her to choose whatever prize she wanted.

She laughed and pointed to the stuffed owl in the top row.

The kid manning the booth used a pole to grab the toy.

He handed her the coveted prize with a flourish. "For you, madame."

"She's going to love it."

He feigned shock. "All that hard work and you're going to give it away?"

"Do you really think I could bring this home and get it past Phoebe?" she asked.

"It's not very realistic. She might reject it."

Rory shook her head. "Not once she learns you won it. She thinks you're awesome."

"Well, the feeling is mutual," he said and realized he meant it.

He was not only falling for Rory but Phoebe had also wormed her way into his heart. Walking around the carnival tonight and having people smiling and nodding at them as if they were a family earlier then later as a couple felt good.

There was a time after his injuries and leaving the army, he'd wondered if he would find that place where he belonged.

Tonight proved he was getting closer to finding it.

"I heard you had a great time last night," Walt said. "Even won something on those midway games."

Mitch was with Walt in the barn. The older man was showing him how to change the tractor's oil.

"I was glad I was able to save face after telling Rory I could win her a stuffed animal." Mitch chuckled. "Took me a few times to figure out which way that blasted rifle pulled."

"What the…?" Walt said, removing his cap and scratching his scalp.

Mitch turned to where the older man was looking.

Sarge came into the barn sporting a bandana fashioned from some sort of hot-pink glittery material reminding him of one of Phoebe's princess gowns. The dog looked first to Walt then to Mitch as if looking for help.

"I'm not sure anything can restore your dignity after this, bud," Mitch told the dog.

Mitch turned to Walt. "Phoebe I presume?"

"Yeah. She likes to dress him up," Walt confirmed. "I have to give the dog credit. He's quite tolerant."

"And obviously color blind," Mitch quipped but knew dogs had blue-yellow dichromatic vision, meaning they saw variations of blues and yellows but not much in terms of red and green. So probably not pink. "And to think he was once a warrior with the 75th."

"Yep. How the mighty have fallen," Walt said with a pointed stare at Mitch's hot-pink silicone bracelet.

Mitch held up his hand as if modeling the bracelet. "You're telling me you wouldn't wear something like this if she gave it to you?"

Walt didn't answer and Mitch snorted. "I thought so."

Sarge sat down in front of Mitch and looked up at him but Mitch shook his head. "I'm sorry, buddy, but if Phoebe wants you to wear it, I think you should."

"See?" Mitch held out his hand. "I'm wearing

the bracelet she gave me. I think we need to suck it up and be good sports."

He rubbed the dog's head. "It's no too much to ask to make a little girl happy, is it?"

Sarge laid down with a sigh and put his head on his remaining paw.

"Now there's a resigned look if I ever saw one," Walt remarked.

Mitch patted the dog on the back. "Good boy."

"Mitch, could you get me a roll of paper towels from the house?" Walt asked, grinning at the dog. "We're all out and I will need some before I finish this oil change."

"Sure. Be right back."

Sarge started to rise but Mitch ordered him to stay.

Walt gave him a look and Mitch laughed. "I don't know what he might come back wearing."

Walt shook his head and laughed and went back to trying to loosen the oil filter.

Mitch approached the house but stopped when he heard voices coming through the screen door.

"The offer still stands."

"And I appreciate that, Curt, but Phoebe totally misunderstood that conversation with Bo. I wouldn't want to confuse her by moving back, no matter how temporary."

Mitch stopped in his tracks. Was she looking to get back with her ex? He knew Phoebe missed her dad. Was he coming between reuniting a family that had been broken apart? Yes, he was definitely attracted to Rory and he was smitten with little Phoebe but he never meant to come between them and this Curt.

He swallowed the bile rising in his throat and wiped his palms on his jeans.

He needed to get those paper towels and bring them back to Walt or the other guy would come looking for him. Should he go in and interrupt?

The voices receded as if they were going towards the front of the house. Mitch went into the kitchen, careful not to let the screen door slam behind him. Maybe he could get the towels and get back to the barn before she realized he was here.

He found what he was looking for and was heading for the door.

"Mitch, I thought you and Walt were in the barn tinkering with the tractor."

Caught. He turned around and stood looking at her, his brain scrambling for something to say.

"Something wrong?" Rory asked, that furrow between her brows quite evident.

He sighed. "I…it's, uh, about your ex."

"What about him?"

"I couldn't help overhearing. I apologize. I should have walked away but I didn't." That alone should concern him. If there was a possibility that she could get back with her ex and create a firm, stable family for her little girl, he needed to step aside. Could he do that and still stay at the farm?

"We weren't discussing anything top secret, so no harm done."

"Is…ah, there a chance you might be getting back together? He invited you and Phoebe to stay with him."

"Absolutely not. Phoebe told Curt about that conversation she overheard between myself and my brother." She frowned. "I didn't realize how upset she was by that innocent conversation. I'll have to reassure her. She's upstairs. I'll go talk to her now unless you needed me for something."

Mitch shook his head and held up the roll of towels. "Just came looking for these. Go talk to her if you need to."

"Thanks," she said, sounding preoccupied about her daughter.

He exhaled and left the way he'd come, using the time walking back to the barn to compose himself.

The prospect of her getting back with her ex had torn him up. Her fervent denial it was never going to happen went a long way to help mend the rift in his heart.

Chapter Thirteen

"Are you ready to read some more from my owl book, Mr. Mitch?"

Mitch finished washing his hands at the kitchen sink and dried them on a towel. "Sure."

It had been several days since the carnival. He and Rory had had to postpone their date at Angelo's because Phoebe had come down with a stomach bug and hadn't wanted to be away from her mother. Mitch couldn't blame the little girl. It was just bad luck it had happened on the weekend of their date.

"Yippee. I'll go get it," she said and ran off.

Phoebe came back into the room with the book that was half as big as she. She held it out and he took it, flipping through the pages to find where he'd left off.

"What are you doing?" she asked him.

"I was trying find where we left off from last time."

"But I want to read about the great horned owl," she said, pointing at the book. "Mommy says it's not a chron-chron-something story where you has to read from the first page to the last in order like with my other books. Do you know that word, Mr. Mitch? You's really smart and good at 'splaining things to me."

He smiled at her but had to press his lips together when they trembled a bit. Before this, he would have said he was the least sentimental guy he knew. He couldn't claim that anymore. This little girl had him re-thinking how he saw himself. He cleared his throat before saying. "I think your mommy was saying chronological and it means just what you said. That it goes from the first page to the last in the order so the story makes a sense."

"But I could read any book out of order if I wanted, right?"

Seems like his little Phoebe was a rebel at heart. Wait… What? *His* Phoebe? She wasn't his. The same way Rory wasn't his. But they could be and how did he feel about that?

"You can read books in any order that you want. Princess."

"The owl you won for me at the carnival is a great horned owl. Did you know that?"

"I didn't at the time, but I have since been reading up on owls. Great horned owls are very sedentary."

"I don't know what that means."

Mitch chuckled. He should have anticipated that. "It means that they're basically lazy."

"But don't they have to go and get food? Even Mommy has to go to someplace to get food."

"Yeah, but when they're not getting food, they like to sit around." He was still grappling with his earlier thoughts about being able to lay claim to she and her mother, being a permanent part of their lives.

She put her hand to her mouth and giggled. "Mommy says I'm lazy when I don't want to pick up my toys. Do you think owl mommies say that?"

"Maybe."

"What else do you know about them?"

"They often stay in a single territory all their life." Before she could say anything, he continued, "That means they don't move away from home."

By joining the army he'd moved away from his boyhood home near Chicago and never returned there to live. Although he'd only been here a short time, Loon Lake was beginning to feel like home, a home he might not ever want to leave.

"Not like me and Mommy did when we came here. But Mommy says this is our home for now and even if we leave Sarge could come with us so that's good. She promised we wouldn't move somewhere without my dog."

"Are you sad that you had to move away from your dad?" Was Phoebe wishing her parents would reunite? Would that be something he'd have to contend with if he became a part of their lives?

"Sometimes, but he still comes and gets me so I

can stay with him. And I like it here now because
Sarge was here." She looked up at him. "And I love
it because you're here."

"Thank you," he said simply, gazing down at the
little girl next to him. Maybe Phoebe's heart was
big enough to include both men in her life. That
thought warmed his heart.

"Why?"

"Why what?" he parroted back with good cheer.

"Why did you say thank you? What did I do?"

"You made me feel better," he told her. And it
was the truth. A child of four had improved his
mood—just like her mother did. Being a part of
their lives had enriched his.

"Like Sarge makes me feel better?"

"I guess so."

"I don't know what I did, but I like making you
feel better. Does Sarge make you feel better too?"

The dog sat at Mitch's feet and looked up ador-
ingly at him.

Mitch carefully hunkered down and rubbed the
dog's head and ears. "He sure does. Don't ya, boy?"

His conversation with Phoebe last week about
owls and homes had been on Mitch's mind ever
since. He'd even taken a drive to the home improve-
ment store a few days ago to pick up some supplies
for a project.

He'd been working on what he was referring to
as his secret project in the bunkhouse in his spare
time and came out now to the barn to put the fin-

ishing touches on it. Several minutes later, Sarge wandered in and sat at his feet.

"Where's your mistress?" he asked the dog as he massaged behind the dog's ears like he knew Sarge enjoyed.

"Does you mean me?"

He looked up at the sound of Phoebe's voice and smiled. "I guess I do. Where's your mom?"

"She's coming. She stopped to check on the chickens but she said it was okay to come in here because you were off the clock. What does that mean? Were you fixing a broken clock?"

"No. That means I'm done working for the day," he told her.

"But it looks like you're still working. What's that?" She pointed to his special project.

"It's called an owl box."

She scrunched her face up. "You mean you're gonna put owls into a box? They might not like that."

Mitch smiled and shook his head. "No. Hopefully they'll go in there all by themselves. No one is going to force them."

"How come they want to go in a box?"

"It's not just a box. It's more like a bird's nest only this is even better. Owls aren't very good at making nests, so this gives them a nice place to sleep and to take care of their owl babies."

Phoebe's eyes grew large—like an owl's, he noted with a grin.

"You mean you're making a house for the birds?" she asked.

"Yeah, I guess you could say that."

"Where are you gonna put it?"

"Well, it's supposed to be at least ten to twenty feet up in the air, so I'll need to find a large tree to attach it to. Unless you or your uncle have a spare telephone pole."

"I don't know what that is."

Mitch suppressed his grin. Phoebe wasn't shy about demanding explanations from adults when she didn't understand something, and he was finding that he didn't mind it. Helping explain something to her sometimes helped him parse out what he meant to say. "Telephone poles are those things you see along the road."

"Why does they gots them?"

"They hold up the wires for electricity, telephones and cable."

"The people that work on them use those trucks with the buckets on them. I saw lots of them after the storms. Mommy says they have to climb up to fixes the wires."

"I'm impressed that you know that," Mitch said. She was a very smart little girl.

Phoebe parked her hands on her hips. "I don't know what impessed means."

He scratched a hand over the back of his scalp. How was he supposed to explain it to her? He'd find a way—he was getting used to having to decipher adult for the kid. "It's how you make me feel when you do a very good thing or show me how smart you are."

"So, you're impessed when I do something good?"

"Yeah, I guess that's it," he said.

"You're like Mrs. Addie. She uses big words too. Teddy, he's lots older than me. He goes to school and everything, but he's still my friend." She gave him a look as if daring him to contradict her. "Teddy says Mrs. Addie is very smart and that's why she works at the liberry. Teddy is really her brother, but he lives with her and Mr. Gabe like they're his mom and dad."

"Are those the people we met at the carnival?" he asked. Rory had introduced him to so many people he had trouble keeping them all straight.

"Radar and Sarge are doggy friends."

He nodded, remembering Gabe was the former marine. "How about if I try not to use too many big words from now on?"

"But then how will I learn them?"

"Well, I…" He scratched his cheek. "You got me there, kiddo."

"If I wants to be a *orange-thologist*, I will need to know lots and lots of big words. Mommy says so. She says I hafta go to school lots and lots."

"I suppose that's true. How about if I use words you don't know, you tell me."

She narrowed her eyes at him. "Isn't that what I just did?"

Mitch couldn't hold back the laughter that bubbled up. She sounded so much like Rory scolding him. And he realized he rather enjoyed the verbal sparring he and Rory sometimes engaged in. His ex and he never had that kind of relationship. Cynthie had expected him to go along with her wants and needs. Most of the time he did just to avoid an argument. But it was more than that. He didn't feel the need, but Rory was different. He wanted to clear the air with her, set things right before they had a chance to fester.

After checking on her chickens, Rory went looking for Mitch and Phoebe in the barn. She hoped Phoebe wasn't getting on Mitch's nerves. He'd been working on some sort of project the past few days. He wouldn't tell her what it was. He said he wanted her to be as surprised as Phoebe.

In the barn she found Mitch and her daughter in a conversation about owls. No surprise there.

As soon as Phoebe spotted her, she ran over and grabbed her hand to urge her forward. "Look, Mommy, Mr. Mitch made an owl box. He says an owl box a house for them and their babies."

The fact Mitch would do something like this for Phoebe threatened to overwhelm her. How could she not fall in love with this man on the spot? Whoa, she needed to step back from the precipice for a moment. Love was a big thing. A big step. Was she ready for something like that?

She admired Mitch's handiwork but the chaotic thoughts bombarded her and she kept sneaking glances at him, hoping her feelings weren't stamped all over her face. Or on her sleeve. Or wherever it was she seemed to wear them.

"It's beautiful but it looks like the paint is still

wet," she said. "Perhaps we should go outside while it dries. I'll be Sarge would appreciate a game of fetch."

Sarge obviously understood that word because he jumped up and woofed his approval of the idea.

So they trooped outside with Sarge to play ball while the paint on the owl box dried safely out of reach of prying fingers.

Phoebe was disappointed when Rory reminded her she was visiting her dad that night.

But Mitch reassured Phoebe. "We need to let the paint dry completely and I have to find a good spot to put up the box."

"How will you know where to put it?" Phoebe asked.

"I guess I'll have to do some research."

"Would an *orange-thologist* know where to put it?" she asked.

"I'm sure they would, but I will look it up on my computer."

"I would know if I was one, huh?" Her lower lip jutted out.

"Yes, but I think we need to put the box up before then, don't you?" he asked gently, glancing at Rory looking for guidance.

"We can enjoy learning all about the owls until then," Rory suggested, giving Mitch a nod of reassurance.

"I guess," Phoebe said, kicking her foot in the dirt.

"And thanks to Mr. Mitch we might even be able

to see some owl babies," Rory said, praying her daughter didn't say anything to hurt Mitch's feelings after his kindness in building the box.

"I guess," Phoebe mumbled.

"I have an idea." Mitch snapped his fingers. "I'll see about ordering a small camera to put up too."

"What will that do?" Phoebe asked, suspicion in her tone.

"If I get a motion activated one, it will take pictures or video of the owl or owl babies," he told her, sounding as if he liked the idea.

Phoebe brightened. "Real pictures just like in my big owl book?"

"Yep, that's probably how they got some of those."

More likely a professional wildlife photographer with an extremely expensive telephoto lens, Rory thought but kept her mouth shut.

"That's better than just drawings like in that owl book when I was a little kid. Remember, Mommy?"

Rory exchanged an amused glance with Mitch. It was only a glance but she felt it down to her toes. Wasn't this the sort of things couples did? Exchanged knowing glances and had inside jokes, stuff that meant nothing to anyone but them.

"Yes, that book only had drawings," she said, realizing both Phoebe and Mitch were looking at her.

"Then that's settled. I'll see what I can come up with by the time you get back," he told Phoebe.

Sarge grumbled as if not enjoying being ignored by all the humans. He pushed his tennis ball toward Mitch, who grinned and tossed it. The dog caught the bright green ball in midair.

Phoebe clapped, jumping up and down, evidently back in good spirits. "I'm impessed. Aren't you, Mommy?"

"Impessed?" Rory asked, wondering what in the world Phoebe was talking about now. As saddened as she was when she thought about her failed marriage, she gave thanks on a daily basis for her precious daughter. She couldn't imagine life without this curious and precocious human being.

"Uh-huh. Mr. Mitch taught me that word. I told him something and he said he was impessed and told me what it means."

Rory could imagine her intrepid daughter putting her hands on her hips and demanding Mitch tell her the definition of *impressed.* Her heart melted at the thought of Mitch having the patience to explain things to her. As wonderful a dad as Curt was, and she had to admit that about her ex because any problems they had didn't extend to their daughter, he sometimes lost his patience with her constant questions and utterances of "why?"

"I wanted to thank you for explaining the definition of *impressed* to Phoebe," she murmured to Mitch.

"No need to thank me."

"I'm sure she can sometimes get on people's nerves with her demands."

"She's four. How could she get on my nerves?

Besides, I admire her thirst for knowledge." He grinned at her—and lit up her whole world with the affection in his eyes.

After Phoebe left with Curt, Rory approached the newly occupied henhouse and wrinkled her nose. "What in the world is that awful smell? I've kept this place scrupulously clean. They never smelled like this when Mary had them."

"I believe the source is right over there." Mitch set the brush down he'd been using to paint plant boxes for Rory.

He hitched his chin toward the dog lazing in the grass about ten feet away.

"Euww, Sarge. What did you find to roll in?"

The dog scrambled to his feet and barked as if defending himself.

"Sorry, bud, but that rank smell is definitely emanating from you," Mitch told him and held up a hand when the Belgian Tervuren took a tentative step toward them. "Stay."

Sarge grumbled low in his throat but lay back down in the same spot, putting his head on his remaining front paw.

Mitch turned to her. "I'll do a perimeter check as soon as I clean up these brushes and let you know."

She made a face. "I'm not sure I *want* to know the details because I fear whatever it was might require a burial."

"I'll take care of it."

"Thank you," she said and heaved a sigh. "I'll get

the hose and Phoebe's kiddie pool and give him a bath."

The dog obviously understood the word bath because he grumbled again.

"Sorry, but if you want to be fit for human company, a bath is a necessity," he told the pup and set the brushes in a pail of water until he had time to properly clean them.

Sarge lifted his head and gave him a *woof* in response.

Rory filled the blue plastic pool with water and set a bottle of dog shampoo next to it. "Okay, get over here and get clean. It's a good thing I love you as much as I do," she grumbled as the animal's scent wafted over her as he climbed into the pool.

He might grumble about the indignity of taking a bath in a plastic pool, but Sarge was too well-mannered to do anything but sit.

Most of the odor was a memory by the time Mitch came back, carrying a shovel and a look of distaste on his face.

"Was it that bad?" she asked, gnawing on her lower lip as she lathered up the dog's shaggy coat.

He shrugged. "Let's just say it's taken care of."

"Thank you." She decided not to pursue it because if she found out what the dog had rolled in as she might just start feeling sorry if some poor creature had come to a bad end. Yes, that was nature but she didn't have to roll in it like Sarge.

She started to reach for the hose, but Mitch grabbed it first. "At least let me help."

"You took care of the other nasty bit I figured I could take care of this part."

The dog looked at her and whimpered, as if he understood Rory's words. "Oh, you big baby, I wasn't calling you nasty, just the smell."

Mitch turned on the hose but Sarge took that moment to move and the water sprayed on Rory instead.

"Hey, watch it," she shouted, jumping back and landing on her butt. But it was too late. She was soaked and Sarge wasn't helping when he shook off, sending water droplets everywhere.

"Oh jeez, I'm sorry. I didn't mean to—"

He didn't get to finish because she splashed the water at him. She decided that she and the dog weren't going to be the only ones soaking wet.

"Hey," he complained and reached for her but slipped and toppled over.

He landed on the ground next to her. She inhaled sharply, fearing he might have hurt himself. She didn't want to be responsible for that.

"I'm so sorry. Are you okay?" She reached out and he grabbed her hand and pulled her on top of him.

"Now I am," he said as he arranged her in a comfortable position.

"I don't want to hurt you." But she was loving this position.

"I think I need some mouth-to-mouth if I'm ever to recover."

"Poor baby. Let's see if I remember the lifesaving course I took," she teased.

She leaned down and touched her lips to his. It was a light, tentative touch but it reverberated, and he deepened the kiss until they were kissing passionately. Nothing tentative about this kiss...or this position.

He pulled away first and glanced around. "Should we take this somewhere more private?"

"Good idea." She sighed in relief. At first she feared he'd changed his mind.

"Bunkhouse?" he asked.

"Yeah. More privacy."

"We have a history of getting caught, don't we?" He laughed. "And that's where the condoms are. Unless..."

"I don't have any and I prefer not getting caught. I'm not ashamed of my feelings but I prefer privacy to express them to their fullest," she said and winced. Talk about sounding like some sort of prude.

Prudish was the last thing she was feeling right now because she wanted nothing more than to rip his clothes off.

"We'd better hurry," he said and scrambled to his feet, holding out his hand to help her up.

She gave him a quizzical look and he grinned.

"Your face is very expressive," he said and took her by the hand and led her to the bunkhouse.

"What about?" she asked pointing at Sarge.

"Stay," he ordered but turned back and mouthed "thank you" to the dog.

"My sentiments exactly," she said.

Chapter Fourteen

Mitch sat down on the bed, his weight depressing the mattress and she rolled closer, laying her hand flat against his back. He reveled in the warmth of her hand against him.

This was the moment of truth. He was going to have to take his pants off in front of her...again. But this time he didn't have anger fueling his actions, no self-righteous outrage on his side. This time he was in control of his emotions. At least he had been until she moved her hand across his back in a broad sweeping motion.

And there went his control. These feelings were almost as uncontrollable as the anger had been. Except these were positive.

She reached up and squeezed his shoulder. "What is it? Second thoughts?"

"No second thoughts about us. It's just..." He sighed, "I'll be taking the prosthetic off."

"And?"

"I..."

"I saw you without your pants before. Remember?"

"How could I forget?" He turned to look at her. "You said I was basic...not very sexy."

"I lied. Your boxer briefs may have been basic but the man that was—*is*—in them is spectacular."

"Spectacular? Aren't you getting a little ahead of yourself?" he said teasingly. "I haven't even done anything yet."

"I'm not talking about sex. I'm talking about you. The person you are," she said earnestly, and his heart raced at the sincerity in her tone. The warmth. The kindness.

"You're just saying that because I won you a stuffed animal at the carnival."

"Okay, I confess, that did influence me." She grinned. "But just a little."

He raised off the bed enough to slip his pants off. *Here goes nothing.*

He used the palm of his hands to roll the silicon sleeve down the front of his thigh, unfolded the sock from over the liner, aware that Rory was watching him.

"Not exactly sexy," he muttered.

She squeezed his shoulder and kissed his cheek. "I want to know everything about you, so that means learning this."

He paused in his actions to kiss her, a tender

meeting of his lips with hers. Pulling away, he said, "Kinda kills the spontaneity."

"There's something to be said for delayed gratification."

"Oh?" He raised an eyebrow and she nodded. Smiling, he said, "I'll take your word for it."

Before removing the liner, he faced her. "It's not too late to change your mind."

She took his hands in hers and made eye contact. "I want you. That means *all* of you, Mitch. It's not going to bother me because it's you. All of it is you."

"You're starting to convince me," he said. More than he'd ever thought possible, this woman was becoming part of him—part of his life, his soul, his heart.

She dropped his hands and cupped his face between her hands and kissed him. She lit a fire within him that only her touch could quench before pulling away and asking, "How's that for convincing?"

He blew out his breath. "It's a start."

"Do you need to take the sock off?" she asked, glancing at his stump.

"Yeah."

"Can I?" She started to remove the protective sock but stilled when he winced. "I don't want to hurt you."

"It hurts but not in the way you're thinking. It's actually sweet torture to have you touching me."

"Good. Then I must be doing something right." She pulled the sock off. "Anything else?"

"Normally, I'd check the skin for any irritations."

"Is that one of the rules you told Phoebe about?"

"Yeah."

"Let me."

Even in his wildest dreams, he couldn't have imagined her light touch would be so tantalizing. The fluttering touch of her fingers shot straight to his groin making him harder than he ever thought possible.

"Everything looks okay," she said and reached for the prosthetic. "Where do you want me to put this?"

"Set it against the nightstand. I'll need it later. Not supposed to walk without it."

"Why not?"

"The blood can pool in the stump and then the sleeve won't fit properly." He knew none of this was sexy but he needed her to understand his reality. All of it.

"So the shape and size can change?"

"Are we talking stump or something else?"

She laughed and swatted him. "Right now we're talking resditual limb. I didn't realize it changed."

"Yeah. After the surgery it was swollen for a long time." That's a bit too much, he thought but he didn't want to sugar coat anything the way he might have with someone else. Rory deserved the unvarnished truth.

"So you're okay with me touching it?"

"Are we still talking stump?" he asked, raising his eyebrows.

She chuckled. "We'll get to that other one soon."

"Thank God." He gave an exaggerated sigh but was enjoying this part as much as the sexy parts.

She touched his thigh again and he groaned. Snatching her hand away, she asked, "Did I hurt you?"

"No but you are torturing me." And he meant it too. He couldn't ever remember feeling this eager to touch another human being.

"Sorry."

He leaned over and kissed her, letting their tongues mingle and spark fire within him. "Don't be."

"What position is comfortable for you?"

"I don't know."

"You don't know?"

His chest expanded until it was painful to breathe. "I haven't...since the operation," he said quietly. Had he gone too far with the truth.

She smiled. "Then we're even because I haven't since the divorce."

He pressed his palm against her cheek and gave her a hard, bruising, and yet cleansing, kiss. They could meet each other where they stood—he loved that.

When she made a noise, he broke the contact but continued to cradle her head in his palms. "I'm sorry. Did I hurt you?"

"No, I'm right here with you." She threaded her fingers in his hair, resuming the deep, passionate kiss between them.

"Why are you still wearing these?" she asked, inserting her fingers under the waistband of his boxer briefs.

"Waiting for you to remove them?"

"Is that a request or an order?" she asked.

"Both?"

"Then lie back."

"Yes, ma'am." He lay back and scooted toward the pillows, so he was lying flat-out on the bed like some sort of sacrifice. "I'm all yours."

"And don't you forget it," she said and tugged off his boxer briefs.

When he sprang free, she reached over. Her touch was gentle, tentative, but his hips bucked under her hands, and he couldn't hold back the groan. Growing bolder, she stroked him, and he gritted his teeth hoping to hold on to his control. They'd gotten this far, and he didn't want to embarrass himself by ending this before she'd even gotten all her clothes off.

"Aren't you a little overdressed?" he asked. Oh God, what if she'd—

She pressed her fingers to his mouth. "Now who's overthinking things?"

He laughed. "Except I don't usually think with my mouth."

"Good because I'm hoping you have better uses for it," she said and pulled her shirt over her head and removed her bra.

"I should have done that before lying down."

She frowned. "Why? Like I said before, I'm capable and we don't have to do things a certain way. We can find our own way."

"What did I do to deserve someone like you?" he asked.

"Luck? Mistaken identity? Chloroform?" she asked, her eyes twinkling with amusement.

He laughed, remembering the conversation from

the restaurant. And whatever he *had* done to deserve her, he definitely wasn't going to second-guess it.

She pulled off her shorts and underwear and snuggled next to him. He pulled her closer, turned on his side and took the puckered point of her nipple into his mouth and sucked.

His wandering fingers found a spot that made her moan and soon had her worked into a frenzy— and himself worked up with desire.

"Oh please," she begged. "Yes, right there."

He applied a little more pressure, and she came apart in his hand.

"Damn," he muttered. How could he have forgotten about the condoms? It wasn't as if he could jump up and dash into the bathroom to get them.

"What? What is it?"

"Condom," he muttered. He should have thought of that first and had it ready. Where was his usual finesse? *There's been nothing* usual *about your life for a long time now*, he reminded himself. Making love with Rory was a totally new experience for him, in more ways than one.

"Where are they?"

"In the bathroom in my shaving kit."

She scrambled off the bed and went to retrieve the condoms. He enjoyed the sight of her bare backside as she went into the tiny bathroom.

"Were you planning a party?" she teased as she came back and held up the box.

"No, but it looks like you might be."

She settled on the bed with the container and took one out. "May I?"

After she got him sheathed, he said, "Do you mind being on top? At least until we get this figured out." He didn't want things to be more awkward than they already were.

"I'm sure you need to be in a comfortable position. And…and whatever happens, it won't change my feelings for you. I hope you understand that."

He blinked to clear his vision. Damn. Where was all that arrogance he'd once possessed? Would Rory have liked that guy? The guy who'd had no doubt he'd make it through Ranger school. The guy who'd taken a lot of things for granted.

"I'll make it good for you, I promise," he vowed.

"Thank you, but I want it to be good for you too." She took his face in her hands and kissed him.

"Kiss me like that and it will be." And it might be over before it started but he kept that to himself.

Mitch held out for as long as he could, wanting to make it last for Rory too. And he managed to get her to fall apart a second time. Closing his eyes, he used his hands to pull her hips down on him one last time before he exploded in a release that bewildered him. He'd never experienced anything this intense even before the amputation. Perhaps if he wasn't so numb with pleasure, he'd be able to figure out why or the implications of what had happened. Why things were so different when he was intimate with Rory than when he'd been with any other woman.

"I'll take care of the condom," she said and did just that.

Another thing he hadn't really thought out. What had happened to all his careful attention to details? He'd known this first time was going to be awkward and he was grateful Rory was his partner. Not just because he had deep feelings for her but because of the type of person she was. Obviously, Cynthie's attitude and rejection had done more damage to his self-esteem than he'd previously thought. Rory was nothing like that, and he couldn't deny how much he'd come to care for her.

She came back to the bed and stretched out next to him. He anchored her against him with his arm and she rested her head on his chest. *This is where she belongs*, he thought.

"Mitch?"

"Hmm?"

"That was amazing." She caressed his chest lightly with her fingertips. "Was it good for you, too?"

"Amazing," he echoed and kissed the top of her head. "I'm glad my missing a limb or lack of finesse didn't scare you away."

"How could it? Mitch, you're not just a leg or a part of one. I'm sorry this happened to you, but it doesn't change who you are or how I feel about you."

"But it did change me," he confessed.

She kissed him again. "But I didn't know you before so you're just Mitch to me. And even if you lost another limb, you'd still be the same guy to me."

A lot of the weight he'd carried for the past year slipped away.

Chapter Fifteen

For the first time in a long time, Mitch's step felt lighter; he felt lighter. If he was a whistler like his grandfather Jim had been, he'd be whistling his head off.

Yes, the sex with Rory had been great but the time leading up to it had been perfect too. He'd felt carefree. Something he hadn't experienced in a long time. It was as if Rory had given something back to him, something he'd been missing since his injuries. He hadn't wondered what she was thinking during their lovemaking because in his gut, he knew she'd been as caught up as he'd been. She'd given of herself freely, without reservation just as he had done.

She hadn't made him feel different, just a guy making love to a woman. When all was said and done, his leg or lack of hadn't mattered to either one of them.

Unfortunately, they hadn't been able to catch more than a stolen kiss or two in the two days following their tryst. Rory had feared coming to the bunkhouse in case Phoebe awoke in the night and needed her for something. She didn't want to have to explain her absence. As for himself, his situation wasn't conducive to sneaking quickly or quietly in and out Rory's bedroom. Just dealing with the prosthesis took time.

This evening he was enjoying sitting in a rocker on the front porch of the farmhouse with Phoebe while Rory took a phone call in the house.

Phoebe was sitting on the top step looking at pictures from a new animal book her paternal grandmother had bought. "Mommy says she's not sure if Sarge would like to have a kitten. I asked my daddy if we could keep it at his house, but he said no. Daddy says he doesn't have time to take care of a kitty."

A kitten? When and how had this happened? Mitch stopped the rocking motion to listen carefully.

Phoebe gave him a speculative glance and he groaned inwardly. He may not have known Phoebe for very long, but he knew what was coming next.

"What about you, Mr. Mitch?" Those big brown eyes seemed to be pleading with him.

How the hell was he supposed to resist? He was finding it harder and harder to resist either of the Walsh women. Damn, when had that happened?

And why would she be asking him? Did Rory already refuse so she was trying her luck with him?

"What about me?" he asked. He might know what the little munchkin wanted, but he didn't have to make it easy for her.

He was still trying to decide how he felt about her turning to him. His feelings vacillated between annoyance that she would turn to him after her mother said no and feeling good that she considered him an important person in her life.

"I thought maybe you could—"

"Phoebe!" Rory appeared in the doorway and stepped onto the porch. "What have I told you about asking for things from Mr. Mitch?"

Had they discussed him amongst themselves? He tried to decide how he felt about that. Numerous emotions bombarded him at once.

"But, Mommy, you didn't say it was a *ru-ule.*"

"I didn't think I needed to, young lady. You should know better than to ask him something like that."

"Why?" Phoebe asked.

"Why what?" Rory lifted her hands, palms out as if trying to understand.

Phoebe scowled. "Why should I know better? You didn't make it a rule. Did you know it was a rule, Mr. Mitch?"

Rory looked to him as if he could provide an answer, but he was doing all he could to contain his laughter. At this point amusement over the entire situation. It was starting to feel bizarre, something that he was familiar with since Phoebe opened the door to him that first day. But he didn't think Rory would appreciate that sort of reaction. Not that he'd blame her. In the end, he shrugged. What else could he do?

"Do I have to make everything a rule?" Rory asked, frustration evident in her tone.

Mitch cleared his throat and both Walsh women looked expectantly at him. "I don't think you need to worry about Sarge harming a kitten, if that's what's bothering you. He's quite disciplined."

"See, Mommy, Mr. Mitch says it's okay if I get a kitten."

"Well, I didn't exactly say that," he clarified but knew it was futile. The damage had already been done. Him and his big mouth.

Rory gave him a look that plainly said, "I'll deal with you later."

Yup, another reason he needed to step back, not get involved as a father figure. He knew nothing about being a dad figure—and he had only *just* become involved with this kid's mom. He could lead men into an urban combat situation without casualties but have a conversation with a four-year-old? And he'd fail.

But she already has a dad, so you don't need to worry about fulfilling that role, a voice in his head reasoned. No, he would be in a sort of a stepparent role…even if he was getting ahead of himself.

"We don't have time for another operation," Rory told Phoebe. "You need to get washed up before Daddy gets here."

They'd spent part of Saturday morning playing board games around the kitchen table. She'd been surprised when Mitch agree to Phoebe's request to join them. He'd been a good sport and managed to let Phoebe win most of the time without making it too obvious.

Rory held out her hand to Phoebe. "Daddy'll be here soon. You don't want to keep him waiting."

Curt was picking up Phoebe for the weekend so she and Mitch could finally go on their date to Angelo's. They'd had to postpone it twice. First because Phoebe had a tummy ache and motherhood took precedence over everything else. Then Curt had had to travel out of town on business.

But tonight everything appeared to be working out. She tried not to dwell on the fact that they'd had sex before going on a date. Unless you counted breakfast or the carnival, both of which had involved Phoebe. She'd had fun on both but they were a far cry from anything romantic like the patio at Angelo's.

"Why can't I go with you and Mr. Mitch?"

Great. All she needed was Phoebe to tell Curt that she'd rather be spending time with Mitch. Technically it wasn't Curt's weekend but he agreed to switch when Phoebe had told him she missed him the week she'd been sick. No matter what went on between them, her ex was a good dad. "Because Daddy is going to take you to supper with your other grandparents. You were excited about it before."

"But I wanna see the submarine races." Phoebe

crossed her arms over her chest and put her hands under her arms.

"The what?" Rory looked to Mitch but he shrugged, seemingly as clueless as she.

"The submarine races," Phoebe repeated. "You and Mr. Mitch are going and I wanna go. Why can't I come too? I'm sure I would like them. I'll go with Daddy and Grandma and Grandpa D some other time."

Rory hunkered down to face her daughter. "Who told you that's what we were doing?"

"I heard Grandpa G tell Mr. Ogle that Mr. Mitch was taking you to a restaurant and then he was gonna take you to the lake so you could watch the submarine races."

It took several moments for Rory to even figure out what Walt must have been talking about. As far as she could tell watching submarine races was a euphemism for necking in a parked car. As a matter of fact there was a spot near the lake that was a kind of a make out spot for teens.

She inhaled to get ahold of herself. On the one hand she wanted to laugh because it was such an outlandish thing and on the other she wanted to strangle Walt for discussing something like that with Ogle Whatley. If Ogle mentioned that to Tavie it would be all over town. There was no "if" about it.

This was almost as embarrassing as the time she did get caught with a boy from school. The cop who'd knocked on the window of the steamed up car had been amused but polite. Of course he'd recognized her because Walt had been with the sheriff's department at that time.

But that's probably why he'd been polite and suggested they move along. Walt had never mentioned the incident directly so all those days of worrying over it had been for nothing but he had, in his way, warned her about teenage boys and what they wanted from teenage girls.

But she'd already given Mitch what they'd both wanted practically from the moment they set eyes on one another. Not that she was going to tell Walt.

Rory heard a choking sound behind her. Ha! Looked like Mitch had put two and two together and figured out the euphemism too. Or he'd used his phone to Google it which she'd been tempted to do.

She didn't dare turn around. If she made eye contact with Mitch, she'd lose control and end up laughing. If that happened they'd be giving too much importance to the subject and Phoebe would never let it go. She'd want to be let in on the joke. She should make Walt explain it to her four-year-old daughter. That would serve him right.

"There are no submarine races, sweetie." What exactly had Walt and Mitch discussed while working on the henhouse? She groaned at the thought that Walt might have asked Mitch's intentions toward her. Would Walt do something like that? What would Mitch have said if he had?

"You're just saying that because you don't want me to come," Phoebe said and gave her a fierce scowl.

Great. How was she supposed to handle this? She was not going to explain to a four-year-old how some dates ended. No way. "Look, Phoebe, I'm telling you that—"

"They were canceled," Mitch said and looked to her for confirmation. "See," he held up his phone, "they told me they weren't having any tonight."

Rory didn't like lying to Phoebe, but like with Santa Claus and the Easter Bunny, she figured this sort of lie wasn't going to harm her development. They'd probably laugh over it someday when Phoebe was old enough to understand it. Maybe when it came time to warn a teen Phoebe what teen boys wanted.

"Rory?" Mitch asked.

"What?" She looked up to see Mitch and Phoebe watching her. "Oh, yes, Mr. Mitch is right."

"Then why did Grandpa G say it?"

Her daughter was nothing if not tenacious. Another thing that would come in handy someday. Rory just didn't want that someday to be now, today. "He probably didn't know they were canceled when he said it, sweetie. Mr. Mitch said he just found out on his phone. Isn't that right?"

He cleared his throat. "Yes, that's absolutely right."

"So let's go get ready for Daddy. You can pick out which dress you want to wear for your date with Daddy."

"My Princess Charlotte dress?"

"If that's the one you want."

Rory thought of the new dress she'd bought for herself. She'd chosen a yellow sundress with a smocked bodice, cap sleeves and a full skirt that fell just below her knees.

Earlier when she'd tried it on, she'd felt every bit the princess Phoebe wanted to be. Would Mitch would like it too?

Mitch was glad he'd taken time to run to the closest mall and buy some decent dress pants and a white button-down shirt for tonight. He'd even invested in black loafers.

Rory was a vision of loveliness. She was beautiful and he told her so as he helped her into his FJ Cruiser.

"Thanks," she said, her cheeks pink.

They chatted about the farm as he drove them through town towards their destination. The restaurant was located on the lake.

At the restaurant, the hostess, a young woman dressed in a white shirt and black skirt, greeted them and Mitch gave them his name. "Ah yes, I see you reserved a spot on the patio. Very nice choice. Everyone says how romantic it is."

Mitch nodded. "That's what I've heard."

He didn't mind if the whole town knew they were on a romantic date. Of course he might want to take Walt to task over his comment about their after dinner activities.

"Right this way," the hostess said and began making her way among the tables.

Mitch took Rory's hand in his and raised an eyebrow when she looked at him. Did she mind everyone seeing them like that? Evidently she didn't because she squeezed his hand and gave him that special soft smile he'd come to associate with her.

They stepped out onto a covered flagstone patio with a pergola strung with thousands of twinkling lights, scattered with tables, and small trees. Tiny fairy lights wound around the trunks and branches of the trees. Each table held flickering candles in glass lanterns.

"It's like a fairy tale," Rory said. "Can you imagine what Phoebe would think."

"Maybe we'll bring her sometime. She can dress like a princess," he suggested and rested his hand on the small of her back as they wound their way through the tables to one overlooking the lake.

"She'd love it."

"But for tonight, you're the only princess I want," he said and pulled out her chair at the table the hostess had brought them to.

He took his seat across from her and accepted a menu. A waiter appeared with water, warm bread, and seasoned olive oil for dipping.

"I'll give you a time to look over the menu and decide," he said and left the table.

"Nice view of the lake," Mitch said before turning his attention to the menu.

"Did you request it special?"

"Wish I could take credit for it but I think it was luck," he said as he gazed at her. "On second thought, they probably saw you and decided you're some undercover princess and gave us their best table."

She blushed. "Or, they saw you and decided you were some Hollywood A-lister trying to lay low in Loon Lake."

He laughed but enjoyed the compliment all the same.

The waiter glided back to their table and took their orders.

After the waiter left, Mitch frowned as he noticed there was a wine list on the table. "Did you want some wine?"

She shook her head and leaned closer. "To be perfectly honest, Two Buck Chuck is about my speed when it comes to wine so anything better would be wasted on me. But if you want some…"

"No, I'm more of a beer guy."

"We couldn't have picked a better night," she said and looked out over the water.

The moon shone down on the lake and reflected off the water, adding to the atmosphere.

"Listen," she said and looked out over the water.

"What? The dog-day cicadas?" he asked above the buzzing sound coming from the trees surrounding the restaurant.

"Well, yes, you can't miss those but every so often you can hear a loon." She sighed. "I just love that sound. It's almost haunting. And I like that they're calling to their mates."

"We can drive to the lake afterward and listen for them."

"I'd love that."

The waiter brought their meals and they busied themselves with eating and chatting about movies and books.

They left the restaurant holding hands.

He suspected Rory believed in fairy tales every bit as her daughter did. Could he give her that fairy tale ending considering his reality? Well, he wasn't going to concern himself with that tonight. He was going to enjoy every moment of being with this wonderful woman. She laughed. "So, you really are taking me to see the submarine races?"

Mitch burst out laughing too. "First time I'd heard it called that."

"They didn't call it that back when you were in high school?"

"Hey, hey, what's this 'back when you were in high school' stuff? There can't be that much difference in our ages." He glanced over at her. "Is there?"

"How old are you?"

"Thirty-two. And you?"

"Six years younger. Not exactly a wide gap. So, you've never heard that?" She giggled. "Or maybe you just didn't do those types of things in high school."

"Oh, I did those types of things." As a matter of fact, he planned on doing those types of things—like necking with his date—once they got to the lake.

At the lake instead of staying in his vehicle, they got out and walked to the end of the public dock.

He put down a blanket he kept in the car. "I don't want you to get your pretty dress dirty."

They sat at the end of the dock, their legs hanging off the edge. He'd probably regret it when it came time to stand up but he was enjoying holding her hand, exchanging kisses, and watching the twinkling stars over the lake too much to worry about anything.

They might have stayed like that most of the night but a flash of lightning brought them to their feet.

"We'd better get to the car before we get caught in the rain," he said.

"Do you need help getting up?"

"I think I can manage," he gritted his teeth and maneuvered himself into a position so he could rise, if somewhat awkwardly.

"It's okay to ask for help," she said. "Look at all the things you've helped me with."

He grunted. Anyone else he might have taken offense but he didn't want to ruin their evening. "I'm okay."

"I'd say you were more than okay, Mitch Sawicki."

He gave her a kiss as the first raindrops started to fall.

The interior lights were on in the farmhouse when they arrived back indicating Walt was home and still up.

"Is he waiting up for you?" Mitch asked.

"I honestly thought those days were over but…"

"But what?"

She sighed. "This is the first date I've had since before my divorce. I'm sorry."

"Because you haven't dated or because he's waiting up for you?" he asked.

"The second one. Definitely the second one. We're adults but…" she let her voice trail off. What was it about parents that made you feel like a kid again?

"It's okay."

"No, it's not," she said and patted his shoulder. "Go to the bunkhouse, I'll talk to Walt and come over."

"Are you sure?"

"It's where the condoms are so yeah, I'm sure."

Mitch laughed and gave her a kiss.

"So, how was the date?" Walt asked as she entered the house.

"The date itself went well. Getting Phoebe to go with Curt to visit her grandparents posed a problem."

Walt frowned. "I thought she was looking forward to it."

"She was until I had to explain to little miss big ears that there weren't going to be any submarine races tonight."

"Subma— Oh. That." Color appeared on Walt's cheeks.

"Yeah. That." Rory put her hands on her hips.

He grimaced. "Sorry. I didn't think she was even paying attention."

"That's your apology? Sorry she overheard instead of sorry I was gossiping about you and Mitch?"

He chuckled. "You're absolutely right. I apologize for talking about your private life. I do not gossip."

"But Tavie does," she pointed out.

"But Tavie wasn't there."

"But Ogle was."

"Point taken." He sighed. "So, what happened with Phoebe?"

"Mitch convinced her they'd been canceled for the evening."

Walt nodded and then broke out into a grin. "And were they?"

Rory sniffed. "As if I would tell a blabbermouth like you."

Walt's laughter followed her as she left the room. She wouldn't let him see, but she was wearing a grin of her own. Partly because she was going to get some toiletries and go to the bunkhouse.

Chapter Sixteen

At the sound of a vehicle in the driveway, Rory stepped onto the porch and waited for the delivery truck to stop.

The uniformed driver jumped out of the truck and jogged over to the porch with a package in his hand.

A week had passed since their date at Angelo's. Although they hadn't managed to snatch a night together, there were a lot of longing glances and casual touches as the passed or talked.

Rory had been extra busy after picking up extra jobs cleaning cottages around the lake as renters came and went. The money she made doing this was welcome and she was able to take Phoebe along with her.

The young man glanced at the box. "Is there a

Mitch Sawicki here?" he asked, slowly sounding out the last name.

"Yes. Do I need to get him?"

"No, it doesn't say signature required. I just wanted to be sure I was at the right place," he said and handed her the box.

Rory took the package and thanked him as he headed back to his white van with the purple and orange lettering. The package was marked fragile and had been sent with overnight delivery. Curiosity got the better of her and she read the return address. Linda Sawicki with a suburban Chicago address. His mother? She had mentioned previously that he should invite her to the farm for a visit. Had he ever done that? She'd love to get to know his family. He knew hers.

She headed toward the barn with his package. He and Phoebe had gone there after breakfast. The plan was to let Phoebe help him paint the owl box he'd made for her. The thought made her chuckle. She'd opted to safely stay in the house for that project.

Well, it looked like she'd get to see how it was going.

"It's bootiful, Mr. Mitch."

Rory smiled as Phoebe's voice reached her as she approached the open double doors to the barn. At least there weren't any tears. Of course, she hadn't seen Mitch yet. The tears could be all on his part.

She walked into the barn. They were at the workbench, and both had their heads bent over a neon pink owl box. Were owls color-blind?

Phoebe spotted her and jumped down from the chair she'd been standing on, then rushed over to Rory. "Look, Mommy, I painted the owl house."

"I see that. At least that owl will know exactly which house is his or hers."

"That's 'xactly what Mr. Mitch said."

Rory met Mitch's gaze over her daughter's head and there was that silent communication between them that she'd been missing from her life. She stood looking into his eyes, thinking how much she enjoyed simply being with him. Sure, the physical side was great too, but talking and being in one another's presence satisfied something she hadn't realized was missing until Mitch came along. She'd been missing a partner in her life. Sure, she had Phoebe and Walt but she didn't have another adult to share certain parts of her life with, things she couldn't or wouldn't share with a parent or a child.

Phoebe had her dad and other male role models in her life so Rory never worried about that, but she herself had no one to be intimate with. No one to share things at the end of the day as the day wound down. No one to talk to after the lights went out. No one to go over the events of the day while lying in the dark.

To find one that was also bonding with her daughter was a bonus. She'd often wondered if she'd be able to find one who would accept that she came as a package deal.

"What's that?" Phoebe reached for the box. "Is it for me?"

Rory held it out of reach. "It is not for you. It's for Mr. Mitch."

She handed it to him.

He looked at the return label and frowned. "It's from my mother."

"You have a mommy?" Phoebe asked.

He laughed. "Believe it or not, I do."

"Is she old?"

"She's about the same age as your grandfather." Mitch took a penknife from his pocket and slit the tape holding the box closed.

"That's kinda old. But is she pretty like my mommy?"

"I'm not sure there's anyone as pretty as your mother," he said and opened the box to reveal a decorated tin.

Phoebe scrunched up her nose and stuck her head over the opened box. "Why did she send this to you?"

"Phoebe, you don't have to know everything," Rory scolded, but had to admit she was just as curious as her daughter to see what his mom had sent.

"I guess it contains something she wants me to have. How about we open it and see what it is?"

He opened the tin to reveal what looked like crispy pieces of fried dough liberally sprinkled with confectioners' sugar.

"What are those?" Phoebe asked.

Rory could see by the look on his face that the gift had thrown him back to another place, another time. If nostalgia had a face, it would be Mitch's at this moment.

He held the tin so Phoebe to see. "They're called chruściki."

"Crushed chicken?" Phoebe tried repeating after Mitch.

"How about we just call them angels' wings?" He laughed and ruffled her hair.

"They look like cookies. Are they cookies?"

"Kinda, but they're also like fried dough." He pulled out a folded piece of stationary that was resting under the tin and read it. "Mom says if they're kept covered in the tin, they'll stay crispy longer. Plastic turns them soggy."

Rory realized that Mitch had an entire other side to him that she didn't really know much about. His upbringing and background. She knew from his last name that he was Eastern European but she'd never thought about what that might mean. Did he have special foods that he liked?

"Mommy and I had fried dough once when we went to the carnibal. I liked it but I was still little so Mommy and I shared it."

Mitch glanced at Rory, and she smiled and said, "Yeah, it was all of last July."

"I'm more growed up now so I don't think I needs to share anymore," Phoebe said and glanced wistfully at the tin of goodies.

"Phoebe, it's up to Mr. Mitch whether or not he wants to share his chru-ch—" She hated that she struggled as much as her four-year-old to pronounce it.

"Crushed chicken." Phoebe supplied for her.

"Thank you, sweetie." She'd have to ask Mitch to share this part of his life with her. Would he want to?

Mitch chuckled and set the note onto the top of the workbench. "Well, that would depend," he said and winked at Rory. "My mother said to share them with my friends and coworkers. Do you think she meant you?"

Phoebe bounced on her toes. "Yes! Me! I'm both."

He held the tin so she could help herself to one. "Then here you go."

After Phoebe chose one, he held the tin out to Rory. Remembering the look on his face when he'd opened the tin, she appreciated him sharing this part of his life with them. Silly because they were only some sweets, but they took on a new meaning knowing how much they meant to him. Would his mother be willing to share some recipes with her?

"Thank you," she said and had to clear her throat before she could continue, "Did your mother make these?"

Phoebe bit into hers and sent powdered sugar flying everywhere.

"Oops. Here. We might need these." He reached across the worktop and grabbed a roll of paper towels. "She always makes them to celebrate the end of the school year. That's what this batch must be for."

Rory took one of the towels he handed her. "Is she a teacher?"

He shook his head. "A school librarian."

Now that was something Rory hadn't known. She felt guilty not asking more questions about his mother.

"Why?" Phoebe asked.

"Why is she a librarian?" Mitch asked.

"No. Why does she make them to celebrate?"

"Tradition."

"I don't know what that means." Phoebe had finished hers and was looking longingly at the tin. Her face was smeared with powdered sugar.

Mitch laughed as if he had expected that. "Well, it's like your Grandpa G taking Sarge to the dog park every Tuesday."

"Huh?"

"Your grandpa doing the same thing every Tuesday is like a tradition."

"And you and your mommy eat the crushed chicken every Tuesday?" Phoebe asked.

"No, just at special times like before Lent or Christmas or weddings. And, of course, the end of the school year."

Rory was soaking up this new information about Mitch, wishing she had asked prior to this. Normally she wasn't selfish but now she felt as if she were.

"You can only has them for stuff like that? Why?"

"Well, that makes them very special. If we ate them all the time, they wouldn't be so special."

"I bet Sarge is glad Grandpa G doesn't take him to the park only on special occasions."

Mitch gave a hearty laugh. "I'm sure."

"What's going on?" Walt came into the barn.

"Look, Grandpa G. Mr. Mitch's mommy sent us some tradition. They're called crushed chicken."

Walt lifted an eyebrow at Phoebe's words. "I have no idea what you're talking about, Munchkin. But whatever it is, it looks as if it attacked you before you ate it."

Phoebe giggled. "You're silly, Grandpa G. The cookies didn't 'tack me, I gobbled them up. Mr. Mitch's mommy made them. He said his mommy is as old as you. She's pretty but not as pretty as my mommy."

"Wow, that old, huh?"

"Have one," Mitch said and held the tin out to Walt.

"Your mom sent them to you and we're all eating them. That hardly seems fair," Walt said but took one anyway.

"They're meant to be shared," Mitch said.

"Is that part of what makes them special, Mr. Mitch?" Phoebe asked and grinned when he handed her another one.

"Yes, it does, Phoebe," he told her.

Rory felt a tingle run up her spine. How could such simple, everyday things feel so special? She glanced at Mitch and had her answer. She wasn't just falling for the guy, but she'd fallen. After telling herself she wasn't going to get involved with anyone until Phoebe was older, she'd gone and fallen for the first man that came her way. How did that make sense?

Mitch set the cookie tin on the dresser. He'd have to thank his mom for the reminder of home.

Home. The word stuck in his mind. Loon Lake was starting to feel like home. Bizarre. He'd had no intention of staying here when he first came but now that's exactly what he was doing. Luckily, he'd been able to contact one of his Ranger buddies to pack up some of his clothes and ship them to him when it looked like he'd be sticking around for longer.

He shook his head at the remembered conversation with Dwayne. His friend had ribbed him asking what the lady's name was. Of course, Mitch had denied the accusation, but as he thought about Rory, he had to admit she was a major factor in his decision to stay in Loon Lake. Oh sure, he got along great with Walt, almost like the father he'd never had, and Phoebe had somehow captured his heart from day one. Maybe her red boots, he thought and laughed.

Glancing out the window, he saw Rory heading to her chickens and he left the bunkhouse to help her round them up and get them secured in the henhouse he and Walt had made by modifying the prefab shed kit.

"Want some help?" he asked as he fell into step beside her.

"You know I can always use help wrangling

chickens." She gave him a warm smile that he felt down to his toes.

"At least they're getting used to the new quarters and are a bit more willing to go inside." Jeez, couldn't he think of something better to say? He leaned closer, enjoying the scent of her hair, as they walked toward the hen enclosure.

"True, but thanks for the help." She bumped shoulders with him, a gesture meant to show without words how she was feeling.

"No problem." And tapped his shoulder back at hers.

Grinning, she turned toward him, her smile and the gleam in her beautiful eyes was his undoing. He was going to wrangle chickens but felt as though he was going on a romantic date instead.

After getting the chickens into their coop and Rory had gone into the house to get Phoebe ready for bed, he stood to watch the glowing sunset. For the first time in a long time, at least since childhood, he was seeing not dust in the atmosphere bending and distorting the sun's light, but the beautiful colors blazing across the horizon felt magical. As if created just for him and this magical moment with Rory. Was he beginning to believe in fairy tales?

Chapter Seventeen

Rory put another egg in her basket. This egg made an even dozen. Not bad from her small flock of chickens. Her hens had all given her eggs today. She'd make everyone omelets tomorrow morning. Mitch had been eating with them for almost every meal, fitting into their family almost seamlessly. She stared into space, thinking about Mitch. He hadn't used the L word with her, but the way he acted made her think his feelings ran deep. As deep as hers? She couldn't be sure.

"Mommy? If you and Mr. Mitch get married, can I call him Daddy Mitch?"

Rory startled and nearly dropped the eggs. Had Phoebe read her thoughts? She and Mitch married? Thinking about this herself, in the privacy of her own mind, was one thing but to have Phoebe bring it out into the open was scary. Even if she'd been thinking along the same lines.

"Ooh, Mommy, look. Another egg. I found it for you." Phoebe held up a brown egg, her smile wide. "So I can call him Daddy Mitch? He'd be like a daddy when you get married."

"You did. Thank you, I almost missed it." Rory took the egg and added it to the basket.

"Yeah, we have to find all the eggs every day, huh?" Phoebe did a little dance twirl.

"We sure do and tomorrow we'll use them for breakfast," Rory said. "What made you think Mr. Mitch and I are getting married, sweetie?"

"Cuz I saw you kissing him in the barn. People who kiss like that get married."

Kissed like that? Oh man, what exactly did Phoebe see? She wasn't setting a good example for her impressionable young daughter. "Just because Mr. Mitch and I kissed doesn't mean we're getting married."

"But I saw you."

"Well, first of all, he would have to ask me. And sometimes people kiss but that doesn't mean they're getting married."

"But if you did, could I call him Daddy Mitch?"

"You would have to ask him that, but I don't—"

"Okay," Phoebe chirped and started skipping out of the barn.

Oh God, what had she done? She couldn't let Phoebe go and ask Mitch a question like that. He'd think she was discussing marriage with her daughter.

"Phoebe, wait!"

She rushed after her daughter.

"Mr. Mitch! Mr. Mitch," Phoebe called and headed in the direction of the bunkhouse.

"Phoebe, don't—"

"Don't what?" Mitch asked, coming around the side of the barn from the other direction wiping his hands on a rag after working with Walt on the tractor.

Rory skidded to a stop, nearly running the poor guy over in her rush to get to Phoebe.

Mitch dropped the dirty rag and grabbed hold of her elbows to steady her. "Careful. What's the hurry?"

Phoebe came back to where they stood, oblivious to the turmoil she had almost unleashed.

"What's going on?" Mitch asked as he dropped his hands but didn't move away.

"Mommy said to ask you—"

"Phoebe, we don't need to bother Mr. Mitch right now." Damn. How had this happened?

"But I wanted to ask him," Phoebe whined.

"Ask me what?" His gaze ping-ponged between the two of them, his brow drawn together in a frown as he picked the rag back up.

"I asked Mommy if I could call you Daddy Mitch when you gets married to my mommy."

"That's a bit presumptuous," he said and looked straight at Rory.

Phoebe scowled, evidently not expecting that answer. "I don't know what that word means. Does that mean you gots some other mommy you wants to marry?"

He shook his head. "Not at the moment, Princess."

"See, Mommy, he doesn't have any other mommies he wants to marry."

Rory wanted the ground to swallow her whole. No such luck so she needed to try and explain. "Mitch, I'm so embarrassed. Phoebe saw...uh, saw something and she got this idea in her head. I never—"

"Consider us even," he said, shaking his head and grinning.

"Even?" She blinked at him in confusion.

"For me humiliating myself by dropping my pants," he said.

"Oh yeah. That." Rory tried to smile but it wobbled. Although his words were said in a joking manner and he was smiling, she hadn't missed the fleeting look of panic that crossed his handsome features at the mention of marriage.

"Yeah. That," he said.

"Mommy?"

Phoebe tugged on Rory's pant leg before Rory could respond to his comments or attempt an explanation. "What is it, Phoebe?"

"I hafta go to the bathroom."

Oh sure, now that she'd wreaked havoc she wanted to go back into the house. Rory sighed. "Alright, we'll go back to the house."

"What you need is a bathroom out here in the barn."

"Yeah, wouldn't that be nice."

"C'mon, kiddo, let's go to the house," she said, reaching out her hand.

Phoebe took her hand and skipped along as they made their way back to the house. She envied her daughter's four-year-old view of the world. Things were pretty simple but grown-up relationships were anything but simple. Love didn't conquer all nor did it solve all problems. If it had, maybe she wouldn't be divorced and Mitch might be with his ex.

Huh, that wasn't the comforting thought it should be.

One thing was certain, she would fight tooth and nail to save a relationship with Mitch.

Mitch watched them walk away. The word *marriage* had been mentioned and he wasn't running for the hills. He wasn't even feeling itchy. Well, maybe just a little tickle.

It was true Phoebe had a biological father present in her life, but since Rory was her main caregiver that meant whoever she married would also be responsible on a day-to-day basis. Was he ready for that? Did he want that? He should be doubly itchy and he wasn't. After the amputation and the breakup, he'd sworn off marriage, but that was before he met Rory and Phoebe. Maybe Cynthie hadn't done as much damage as he'd previously feared. When they'd been engaged he had wanted kids, so why not now? He was certainly smitten with Phoebe and he wouldn't mind at least one or two more. But was he asking for more than he could handle? It had taken nearly a full year to get back to where he was now, feeling good about himself. Could he handle the ups and downs of family life?

When he got back to the house there was a late-model sedan parked in the front. Mitch slowed his approach when he heard voices coming from the porch.

"Phoebe said you and this Mitch were getting serious," a man said.

Mitch had been going to walk away and give them their privacy, but after hearing that, he couldn't pull himself away. Damn, when had he turned into such an eavesdropper?

"Do you have a problem with that?" Rory asked.

"Should I?" the man asked.

"Look, Curt, I'm not going to discuss Mitch with you. It's none of your business."

"If it involves my daughter, it's my business," the man's voice had risen.

"If it gets to that point, I'll let you know. Until then, that topic is off limits."

Mitch swallowed. Did Rory not feel there was anything really significant going on between them? Or did she just not want to discuss it with her ex? And which did he want it to be? He'd had some doubts of his own so why would he not want Rory to feel the same? If he felt conflicted, why shouldn't she?

"Well, Phoebe is quite taken with him. It appears he shares her love of owls."

Rory chuckled. "Let's just say Mitch *indulges* her love of owls."

"What exactly does he do for a living? Certainly he has a real job. Phoebe said he builds owl houses and chicken coops."

"He was recently discharged from the army."

"Oh?"

Rory heaved a heavy sigh. "He was an Army Ranger."

"Impressive," the man said in a tone that implied otherwise.

"Yes, he is. Where are you going with this, Curt?"

"If this guy is going to be in your life, that means he'll be in my daughter's life too. I want to know more about him."

"That's fair enough. Like I said, if there comes a point where you need to know, I will tell you."

"I don't want to see you hurt, Rory. Either of you."

"And I appreciate that. I really do. Did you want anything else?"

"No, I need to get to work."

Mitch heard a car door slam and an engine rev up. He was going to go around back to the kitchen entrance, unsure if he wanted to admit to Rory that he'd listened to a conversation with her ex. Again.

Before he could leave, the front door opened and footsteps sounded on the porch along with the clicking of dog nails.

"Did Daddy leave?" Phoebe asked.

"Yes, he did," Rory answered with a sigh.

"I told Daddy all about Mr. Mitch."

"I know that, sweetie."

"Did I do a bad thing, Mommy?"

"Of course not, sweetie. You can tell Daddy and Mommy anything."

"What about Mr. Mitch?"

There was a pause and Mitch found that he wanted to know the answer as much as Phoebe. He rubbed his chest. What was he getting himself into here?

"Him too," Rory said.

Mitch thought about leaving but Sarge barked and galloped toward him so he accepted his fate. After greeting the dog, he came the rest of the way around to the front of the house. He realized he was going into this without a plan or digesting any of what he'd overheard. But from the moment he'd left Fort Bragg, he'd been winging it. Why stop now?

Phoebe spotted him next. "Mr. Mitch. Mommy says I can tell you anything."

"She did?" He tried to act as if he hadn't just heard what was said but when Rory looked at him, her eyes were narrowed. Did she suspect he'd overheard? He cleared his throat. "Was there something you wanted to tell me?"

"I told my Daddy that if you gots married to us I wanted to call you Daddy Mitch. Mommy says I didn't break a rule."

He had trouble swallowing. Was marriage something Phoebe was imagining or had Rory said something to her. He didn't think so but either way, how did he feel about this? It wasn't the first time he'd contemplated the possibility, but the actual prospect of it didn't horrify him, he admitted.

"Mr. Mitch?"

Fully aware Rory was watching them, he looked down at the little girl and his heart took a tumble. "If, and I'm not saying it's going to happen, but if, then you could call me Daddy Mitch."

"I like that. Because I already call my daddy Daddy so I would need something else to call you so I don't get mixed up. Mommy and Uncle Bo call Grandpa G Uncle Walt, but he said it's okay if I call him Grandpa. I have another one too so I call one Grandpa G and the other is Grandpa D."

"I'm sure that helps avoid confusion. Do you understand what that means?"

Phoebe laughed. "Yeah. I always tells you when you say stuff I don't understand."

"Yes, you do and I'm glad."

Phoebe turned to her mother. "Can I go with Sarge to look at the chickens now?"

"Sure, but don't open the gate. I don't feel like chasing hens around the yard."

"Sarge and I could help you round them up."

Rory shook her head. "Those girls would be so upset we wouldn't even have to use a whisk to beat the eggs before scrambling them."

Phoebe giggled, her bony shoulders going up and down. "C'mon, Sarge, we're gonna go look at them."

She put her arm around the dog and told him. "You heard Mommy. You can't scare the chickens otherwise Mommy will have scrambled eggs."

Sarge made a noise as if he was agreeing and they both trotted off.

After they'd left, Rory turned to him and groaned. "I'm so sorry if she put you on the spot."

He put his hands on her shoulders and urged her closer. "She didn't put me on the spot. I'm honored that she's accepted me. I have a feeling you couldn't be with anyone unless your daughter accepted that person too."

"At her age, she's been through a lot with the divorce, and I never want to bring people into her life on a temporary basis. It wouldn't be fair."

"I agree and I admire your dedication."

"I'm not sure it's dedication or anything to be admired, just feels right."

"And us? Does that feel right?"

She swallowed, her throat muscles working. "It does."

As much as he enjoyed hearing this, the hairs on the back of his neck stood up. Was he ready for this next step in his life? Did she know what she might be getting into with him?

him?" she finally managed to get out before her throat closed completely.

"Pardon? I— Oh dear God. No, no, no. I'm so sorry. That's not why I'm here." The man alternated between imaginative cursing and apologizing. "I'm here looking for Sergeant Sawicki. Mitch Sawicki. Brody Wilson said I might find him here."

"Something's happened to Mitch? But I don't understand. He's no longer in the army."

"I'm not here for any sort of notification. I'm not part of any notification team. I swear."

"You're not?" She did her best to control her breathing. In and out. It sounded like such a simple task, but she was having trouble with it.

"Take a deep breath. That's it. Through the nose." He did it with her. "One, two, three, four, five, six and release through your nose."

She followed his instructions. And found now that she could breathe, his uniform was army, not navy. Something she should have noticed right off the bat, but that hadn't penetrated her frantic thoughts. Besides, the notification team was usually comprised of equal or higher rank of the deceased. She noticed this young man's stripes didn't equal or outrank her brother's lieutenant's stripes.

"Again, I apologize, ma'am. I didn't realize you had a family member serving or I wouldn't have worn the uniform. I was wearing it because I flew standby, and it sometimes helps getting a seat. I'll only be here a couple days and didn't want to waste it waiting for a flight. I haven't changed out of it yet." He looked embarrassed by the admission.

Now that she knew this visit didn't concern Bowie and as far as she knew he was safe, she was able to concentrate on the conversation. At least Mitch hadn't been wearing his uniform that day, so she hadn't embarrassed herself in front of him as she had just done. Still, this visit felt a lot like déjà vu and she got a knot in the pit of her stomach.

"Could you tell me what it is I can help you with?"

"I was looking to speak with Mitch."

"I'm afraid he's not here right now," she said as that uncomfortable feeling grew. "If you'd like to give me your name, I can take a message for him."

"Oh, then I assume he's been reunited with Sarge. I wanted to let him know that the dog had been through rehab and was considered safe to be placed in any family setting."

"Yes, that's been all sorted out," she said. Bowie would never have brought the canine in contact with Phoebe if the army veterinarians hadn't cleared him.

"Great. Tell Mitch I'm glad he's getting his dog back. I'll be staying for a few days with Brody Wilson at his place and I'd like to get together with him. I don't know if you know Brody."

"Yes, I know who he is. Did you serve with Brody?"

"I did, ma'am."

"And Mitch?"

He chuckled a bit and shook his head. "No, ma'am. He was a Ranger."

She could hear the awe in his tone. "But you knew him."

"Everyone in my unit had heard of Sawicki and his dog. Their job was to go ahead and make sure it was safe for the guys bringing up the rear."

The young man apologized again for scaring her and was heading back to his car.

"Wait. Do you know my brother too? Lieutenant Bowie Griffin. He's a...um, he's Navy Special Forces."

"No, ma'am. We didn't cross paths with any SEALs."

"So, Mitch and he wouldn't have worked together?"

"No, ma'am. They weren't in the same place at the same time as we were." He laughed. "We'd sure remember those cowboys. Was there a reason you needed to know? I can—"

"No, that's okay, thanks."

He smiled and tipped his head. "My pleasure."

Rory watched the car as it got smaller and smaller, her heart still banging inside her chest.

Later that evening, she went in search of Mitch and found him in the barn tinkering with mounting the small motion sensitive camera he'd bought onto the owl box.

Seeing him doing that task and knowing he was doing it for Phoebe gave her pause. Did she want to rock the boat and question him about knowing

Bo? She understood, accepted, and forgiven his not saying anything at first about being Sarge's handler. She understood he'd come to get the dog back but he hadn't tried to take Sarge away from Phoebe. He wasn't without principles.

Mitch glanced up when he sensed movement. Rory was standing in the doorway staring at him, looking as if she was trying to decide something.

His gut tightened. Something told him—maybe it was the look on her face—that he wasn't going to like what she had to say.

"Someone came looking for you today. A young man— Oh God," she placed her hand over her mouth and stared for a moment before dropping it to continue, "I never asked him his name. How rude of me."

Mitch carefully set down the tools he'd been using. This wasn't going to be good.

"He had some interesting things to say about you and Bowie."

"I'll bet he did," he muttered under his breath. He should have come clean a long time ago. And what if he had? Would that have changed anything? He should have known a woman like Rory might pretend his circumstances, his missing leg, his not knowing what or where he belonged since leaving the army didn't matter, but in reality, they did. They mattered very much.

"You made me believe you knew Bowie personally." Her emotions were still on the surface from the scare she'd had earlier.

"I never actually said that I knew him," he hedged despite knowing it was the wrong tact to take.

"You made me think you knew him by insisting he'd done you a favor. You even said he'd done you a solid, I think were your exact words."

"Are you keeping track?"

"Maybe I need to if you're going to be lying to me," she shot back.

"I didn't lie about him doing me a favor." *Keep digging, Sawicki, the top of your head is sticking out of the hole.*

"What sort of favor did my brother do you if you two had never met?"

"He adopted Sarge and gave him a good home and a family that loves and cares for him." Well, that was the truth at least.

That stopped her. She looked as if she was trying to decide how she felt about that.

"But I guess you think I'm just one big liar."

"I don't like being lied to even by omission. You knew I had assumed you two knew one another," she stated.

"You made the assumption. How am I responsible for that?" Why was he making this worse? Why was he giving her a reason to end what was just beginning?

"Curt said the same thing when I accused him of letting me think he'd renewed our insurance when he hadn't. What is it about me that allow men to think they can lie to me and get away with it? Do I have *sucker* tattooed across my forehead?"

The fact she was lumping him in with her ex angered him. It hurt to think she could dismiss all he'd done with a wave of the hand. "I didn't say anything because I wasn't sure if your dog was my dog. I needed to see his ear tattoo."

"I would have thought you would have known him without having to look at some number on his ear."

"I knew it in here," he pounded his chest where his heart was. "But after believing he was dead for so long, I was afraid I was fooling myself with wishful thinking."

"Okay, I can understand that, but why let me go on thinking you knew my brother? Why do that?"

Yeah, why do that?

Because he'd desperately wanted to stay even if he hadn't been willing to acknowledge that to himself at the time. But now all his protective instincts were surfacing full force.

Looked as though he'd forgotten his promise to live a selfish life, to not let himself be vulnerable again.

Anger crashed over Rory like a tsunami. This was exactly how Curt had treated her! What had made her think Mitch was different? Somewhere in the back of her mind a tiny voice said he was, but she viciously silenced it. She needed to protect herself, her heart from any more battering.

"You've been lying from the beginning," she accused.

"Well, I never actually said—"

"No!" she shouted. "You don't get to do that."

"Do what?"

"Wriggle out of it by saying it was just an omission. I don't care what you call it, it's still a lie. You lied to me."

He winced. "So what if I did? Did it really matter? It wasn't as if you were willing to give up Sarge."

"He was never mine to give. I told you Bowie was the one who came home with him but he saw immediately that the dog and Phoebe belonged together."

"And I understand that. Once I saw how much Phoebe loved that dog, I couldn't have taken him away from her. Is that who you think I am? A thief as well as a liar?"

"I don't know because I find I don't even know who you are," she practically yelled. Her fear from the soldier's visit mixing with her anger. And yes, she may as well add fear to that cocktail. She was losing her heart to Mitch and it scared her. Fear was making her irrational.

"How can you say something like that?" he demanded, looking hurt.

How could he look hurt? He was the who'd been lying, deceiving them all.

She steeled herself against that look on his face. "I can say it because it's the truth. You've lied to me from the start, even deceiving my four-year-old. Pretending you came to see my brother about a favor he did you. You've never met Bowie."

"I said he did me a favor and it's the truth."

"And even if you consider him adopting Sarge a favor, you came to take him away!" she exclaimed. "That's why you came here. Can you even admit that?"

"Of course I admit it. It's the truth, but as I said, I did that before I met any of you. Before I knew the story. All I had to go on was seeing Walt with Sarge in a YouTube video."

She was confused until she figured out he was talking about the news story of the Sarge preventing a purse snatching. "So, you would have taken Sarge from Walt? And, by extension, me and Phoebe?"

"You say taken like I was going to steal him. I would have told Walt the situation and hoped he'd see reason and let me take Sarge home with me."

"Where he belongs?" she accused.

"I didn't say that."

"You didn't have to," she said. "Because from where I'm standing you want it all."

"What's that supposed to mean?"

"You want it all...you w-want the dog and—Never mind," she mumbled. She's almost said he wanted her but she didn't know that for sure and that's what hurt. When he lifted an eyebrow, she hurried on, "Correction, you only want the dog so you only pretended to want me."

"Is that what I did?"

Please deny it. Tell me it's not true. Make me be-lieve you really wanted me.

But he didn't. He just stood there, a muscle twitching in his jaw. Yeah, she should've known this was too good to be true. A great guy who wanted her and her daughter.

"I'll leave instruction for Walt to finish this and hang it up," he said quietly, pointing to the owl box and camera.

"Why? Where are you going?"

"Leaving. I don't stay where I'm not wanted."

Panic slammed into her full force. "I never said you weren't wanted here."

Stay, fight for what we had. Please.

He looked her in the eye. "Maybe *I* don't want to be here."

She watched him walk out of the barn. Her first impulse was to run after him, apologize for getting so angry. But what would she say?

She searched her brain for a reason to go to the bunkhouse. His wages! She owed him for the past week.

By the time she made her way to the bunkhouse he was loading his belongings into his car.

He stopped and looked at her.

"I..." she gulped, "I owe you for last week."

He stared at her for a moment, his green eyes filled with an expression she couldn't decipher.

"Keep 'em," he said and slammed the rear door shut. He glanced around. "Looks like you need them more than me."

His jab at her attempts to turn the place into

something pierced her heart and she abandoned her plan to beg him to stay.

She stood and watched his taillights disappear, knowing the best thing in her life just drove away.

"And it's all your fault," she muttered to herself.

Later that night when Walt came home from his weekly poker game she was sitting in the kitchen, staring at a cup of coffee that had cooled and congealed.

"What's wrong?" he asked after taking one look at her and pulling out a kitchen chair.

"Mitch left. He says he's not coming back and he b-broke my heart."

Walt studied her for a moment before saying, "I'm going to hunt him down and—"

"Don't you dare harm a hair on his head."

Walt's eyes narrowed. "Oh?"

"I mean—" She heaved a tired sigh. "I mean… oh… I don't know what I mean."

"How about if I just try to talk some sense into him?"

"But this is my fault too."

"I never said it wasn't."

"What if he doesn't want to listen? He might want to wash his hands of me."

"A guy as in love with you as Mitch won't give up so easily. Oh, sure, he might stew for a bit, but he'll come around."

"Are you sure?"

"And if he doesn't, I can still pound that sense into him."

"You'd both love that, wouldn't you?"

"I can still hold my own in a fight."

"Well, you two aren't going to fight. You hear me, Walt?"

He patted her shoulder. "Why don't you tell me exactly what you're talking about."

She explained what had happened, not leaving out any details. This was all her fault. She needed to own it.

"You realize the two of you didn't fight over the dog or whether he knows Bowie." He patted her hand.

"What are you talking about? Of course we did. That's what the whole argument was about." Even as she was denying it, she had a feeling Walt was right. What they fought over was inconsequential and but they'd acted as if it had been life changing.

He shook his head. "You're both using that poor dog as an excuse to break up."

"How do you figure that? Why would we do that?"

"Because you're both frightened." Walt sighed and scratched the back of his scalp.

"Frightened? Mitch doesn't scare me. He's not a violent man." She defended Mitch because she realized she her feelings for him frightened her.

Walt held up a finger. "I didn't say *Mitch* scared you."

"Then what are you saying? What am I supposed to be so afraid of?"

"Your feelings for him are what's got you running scared."

Walt was absolutely right and it made her mad. "And when did you get to be such a relationship expert?"

"I'm not but I've led a lot of guys into battle and I understand how fear can manifest."

She sighed. "So what should I do?"

"At least give the guy a chance. I knew from the beginning that Sarge was his and believe me, I would have fought him if he'd tried to take that dog away from Phoebe. But he didn't and I found myself liking the guy despite his misleading us."

"Hey, what happened to 'I'm gonna hunt him down and pound some sense into him'?"

"I still might do that. Talk some sense into him," Walt said.

Talk? Yeah, right. She shook her head as her uncle walked out of the room. An apology was in order. And if that didn't work? She'd think of something. She was going to live the rest of her life without Mitch. That possibility was too sad to even contemplate.

The next morning Mitch entered Aunt Polly's. Trudi pointed to a booth by window. His booth. Their booth, he amended to himself.

He came here to try and decide what to do. People nodded and smiled as he past. Evidently word hadn't traveled yet about what he'd done. Why had he even argued with her? Did he want to patch things up or just leave town?

Sighing, he settled into the booth and tried to smile when Trudi brought him a coffee.

"Where's the rest of the family?" she asked as she poured the hot liquid into the mug.

"I'm alone this morning."

"Good. Then I won't be taking anyone's seat," Riley Cooper said and slipped into the opposite side. He already had a mug of coffee with him.

Mitch lifted an eyebrow. "Been waiting for me?"

"You could say that." Riley took a sip of coffee.

"How did you know I'd be in here?" Mitch doctored his coffee with cream and sugar.

Riley shrugged. "I guessed you might be here since you didn't check out of the motel."

"So you thought you'd come and escort me out of town? Who sent you?"

"Nah," the other man said and took another sip. "However, I did come to talk some sense into you."

"How did you even know about—Walt."

"Yep. He called me first thing."

"And he asked you to do what? Arrest me?"

Riley chuckled. "If I thought it might put some sense into you, I might. Figured I'd try talking first. Me and Meg didn't stick after the first attempt... well, no, technically it was our second attempt but that's not important. What is important is that I decided throwing away the best thing that had ever happened to me was foolish."

Mitch nodded. Rory and Phoebe were the best

thing that had ever happened to him. "You said last time you never regretted your decision to stay."

"And I stand by that. My brother-in-law told me his dad set him straight when he was about to mess up because he was afraid Ellie's cancer might return. Liam said his dad, who happens to be my father-in-law, asked him if Ellie was more important than his fear. He couldn't have both. I just wanted to offer you some options so you'd make a good choice. The right choice."

After his little speech, Riley rose and threw some bills on the table. "Coffee's on me. Think about it. Oh, and Walt took little Phoebe and Sarge to the park so Rory's alone on the farm."

Chapter Nineteen

Whatever warmth and respite the world had to offer him came from to him through Rory. That warmth was inside Rory. He'd forever be in the cold if he had to live his life without her. He could only pray that he could earn her forgiveness.

He threw some bills on the table with Riley's and went to his truck, heading straight for the Griffin farm. He couldn't give up without a fight. Rory was too important to him.

Yes, he was scared because she came with a ready-made family but he wanted to be with her more than he was frightened.

Huh, maybe Cooper's father-in-law was onto something with his advice.

Mitch found Rory in the chicken coop, tossing feed from a bucket as the hens clucked and swarmed around her. He'd never seen such a wonderful sight.

But when he got closer, he saw that her face was blotchy, her eyes red and puffy. Those details pierced him until he nearly doubled over in pain. He was responsible for that.

"Rory," he whispered, trying to deal with the pain caused by knowing he'd made her cry.

She startled and dropped the bucket, sending the hens scurrying in all directions. "Mitch?"

He started toward the gate but she held up her hand and he stopped in his tracks, his stomach dropping to his knees.

"I'll come out," she said.

She came through and secured the gate. "It'll be easier to talk without those girls milling about."

"Do they gossip as much as the residents of Loon Lake?" he asked, hoping to lighten the mood a bit.

She smiled. "Worse, but you can't always believe what they say."

Relieved, he returned her smile. He wished he had the right to pull her into his arms but knew he needed to earn it. If that called for some groveling, then so bit. Pride was cold comfort without Rory.

"Want to come into the kitchen?"

She was inviting him inside. That had to be good. "Sure."

"I made muffins this morning. Have you had breakfast?"

"I stopped at Aunt Polly's but didn't eat."

She gave him a quizzical look.

He shrugged. "Riley Cooper and I had a little chat."

"Uh-oh," she said and looked him up and down. "Are they all internal bruises?"

"The only thing he gave me was advice."

They went into the kitchen and he sighed. He'd been afraid that he might not see it again. She washed her hands at the sink and pulled out a tin of muffins and the coffee carafe. He washed his hands and pulled out the plates and mugs.

They sat at the table in silence for a few minutes while they ate the muffins.

"I wanted—"

"I should—"

He held his hand toward her, palm out. "You first."

"I said some stuff that I probably shouldn't have," she told him.

"I'm sure I did too." He reached for her hand and entwined his fingers with hers. "Are we going to let words come between us? Why are we giving words that much power over us?"

He squeezed her hand. "I pray that you'll accept my apology. But whatever you decide, you should know, my heart is yours to heal or to break. The choice is yours, Rory. My heart belongs to you today, tomorrow, always. No matter what you decide."

"I want to believe that, Mitch. I really do."

"Tell me what's still troubling you. Let's try and

make words heal the breach this time instead of letting them come between us."

"I don't want to fail again."

"So you don't even want to try? Are you willing to give up before we even try to make this thing between us work out?" He understood her hesitancy. After all, after he and Cynthie broke up, he hadn't wanted to try again. "I understand. I honestly do. After my ex broke up with me I was ready to throw in the towel. I was going to live a wholly selfish life."

She laughed. "You're one of the most giving men I know. What happened to that plan?"

"I met this little princess who scolded me on introduction etiquette, but that didn't convince me."

"No?"

He shook his head. "No. What convinced me was meeting her mother, Princess Aurora."

She blushed and he lifted his free hand to her cheek, cupping it gently, feeling the warmth of her flushed skin.

Staring directly into her eyes, he said, "I love you."

Hope fluttered in her chest, skittish and a bit shy like the hummingbirds that flocked around her feeders. She tried to dampen it, but like those tiny birds who flew great distances on their migratory routes it had stamina. "Honestly, Mitch, I'm scared."

"Of me?"

"Of the future, of making another mistake. When my marriage ended, I took on all that guilt."

"I know you, Rory. The dissolution of your marriage couldn't have been all your fault."

"I know that, but some of the guilt came from not loving Curt enough."

"And now?"

"Whatever you might believe about me, believe this. I love you, Mitch Sawicki, more than I ever thought possible."

"And I love you. I love you enough to take another chance at being a couple. I'm not saying I can promise that everything will be smooth sailing ahead, but I can promise one thing. Without a doubt."

"What's that?" she asked, tears shimmering in her big brown eyes.

"I'm going to love you to the best of my ability for the rest of my life." He took their entwined hands and placed them against his chest so she could feel his heartbeat. "This belongs to you. Nothing you do or say will change that. And I know Phoebe already has a biological dad, but I want to be the best Daddy Mitch that I can. I'll love her as if she were my own and I hope we can give her some brothers or sisters someday."

"You mean that?"

"With everything that I am. I'm sorry I wasn't truthful at the start. You have to believe I would never do anything to hurt you or Phoebe. Even Walt. You're my family now. When I came looking for

Sarge, I had no idea what I'd find. I was expecting Walt or Bowie. I thought I'd be able to explain how I felt about losing my partner. Instead, a tiny princess with red rubber boots and an aluminum foil crown answered the door. Her mother wasn't so bad either. Threw me for a loop even though she wasn't dressed like a princess."

"You must've thought you'd dropped through the rabbit hole."

He threw his head back and laughed. "Exactly."

Epilogue

3 Months Later

Rory reached over and switched off the bedside lamp, plunging the bedroom into darkness. She scooted under the covers and snuggled next to Mitch.

"My mom really likes you," he said, tucking Rory close to his side as they lay in bed.

"I really like your mom." Rory rested her head on his chest. She loved listening to his heartbeat. It was steady and reassuring, just like he was. "Only I'm a bit confused over what to call her."

"She asked you to call her Linda, didn't she?" He rubbed her arm.

"I meant is she my future mother-in-law or my new stepmother now that she and Walt are married?"

"Yeah that makes Walt my stepfather and future

father-in-law since you regard him as a father." He chuckled, sending erotic shivers down her spine. "Maybe we'll just introduce them the way Phoebe does...as Grandpa and Grandma G."

"Good idea. You're such a smart man."

He gave her a squeeze. "We Sawickis know how to pick good life partners."

"I'm so happy that your mom asked Phoebe to be a flower girl. She was bursting out of her skin because she so proud walking down the aisle." Rory trailed her fingers across his stomach. "I guess it's a good thing she'll most likely have outgrown the red boots when it's our turn."

"Bite your tongue, woman. I love those boots," he teased.

Rory playfully swatted him. "At least your mom was a good sport about the boots. The tiara too. Of course, you're the one to blame for that tiara."

"Hey, I offered to buy you one too."

"You're nothing, if not generous." She smiled into the darkened room. This is exactly what she'd been missing. Someone to share things with at the end of the day.

They'd decided since this was a first marriage for both Linda and Walt, they'd hold off a bit for their nuptials. Opting for a wedding in the spring, but they'd taken the plunge and moved in together at the farmhouse while waiting for their own home to be built on a plot of land they'd bought adjacent to Bowie's farm. Walt and Linda were renovating and winterizing a lakefront cottage they'd fallen in love with last month.

She glanced at the glowing clock dial. "The newlyweds are probably landing in Honolulu about now."

"Yeah, I..." he trailed off and groaned.

"What? What's wrong?" She lifted her head to peer at him in the dark.

"Our parents are on their honeymoon," he said.

"So? I—oh, well, let's not think about that."

"And how do you propose we do that, Princess Aurora?"

She giggled. "I can think of a few ways to distract you."

"I like the sound of that," he said and began kissing her.

* * * * *

*Don't miss the previous entries in
Carrie Nichols's Small-Town Sweethearts series:*

The Hero Next Door
The Sergeant's Matchmaking Dog
The Scrooge of Loon Lake
His Unexpected Twins
The Sergeant's Unexpected Family
The Marine's Secret Daughter

Available now from Harlequin Special Edition!

#2959 FORTUNE'S DREAM HOUSE

The Fortunes of Texas: Hitting the Jackpot • by Nina Crespo

For Max Fortune Maloney to get his ranch bid accepted, he has to convince his agent, Eliza Henry, to pretend they're heading for the altar. Eliza needs the deal to advance her career, but she fears jeopardizing her reputation almost as much as she does falling for the sweet-talking cowboy.

#2960 SELLING SANDCASTLE

The McFaddens of Tinsley Cove • by Nancy Robards Thompson

Moving to North Carolina to be a part of a reality real estate show was never in newly divorced Cassie Houston's plans but she needs a fresh start. That fresh start was not going to include romance—still, the sparks flying between her and fellow costar Logan McFadden are impossible to deny. But they both have difficult pasts and sparks might not be enough.

#2961 THE COWBOY'S MISTAKEN IDENTITY

Dawson Family Ranch • by Melissa Senate

While looking for his father, rancher Chase Dawson finds an irate woman. *How could he abandon her and their son?* The problem is, Chase doesn't have a baby. But he does have a twin. Chase vows to right his brother's wrongs and be the man Hannah Calhoun and his nephew need. Can his love break through Hannah's guarded heart?

#2962 THE VALENTINE'S DO-OVER

by Michelle Lindo-Rice

When radio personalities Selena Cartwright and Trent Moon share why they've sworn off love and hate Valentine's Day, the gala celebrating singlehood is born! Planning the event has Trent and Selena seeing, and wanting, each other more than just professionally. As the gala approaches, can they overcome past heartache and possibly discover that Trent + Selena = True Love 4-Ever?

#2963 VALENTINES FOR THE RANCHER

Aspen Creek Bachelors • by Kathy Douglass

Jillian Adams expected Miles Montgomery to propose—she got a breakup speech instead! Now Jillian is back, and their ski resort hometown is heating up! Their kids become inseparable, making it impossible to avoid each other. So when the rancher asks Jillian for forgiveness and a Valentine's Day dance, can she trust him, and her heart, this time?

#2964 WHAT HAPPENS IN THE AIR

Love in the Valley • by Michele Dunaway

After Luke Thornton shattered her heart, Shelby Bien fled town to become a jet-setting photographer. Shelby's shocked to find that single dad Luke's back in New Charles. When they join forces to fly their families' hot-air balloon, it's Shelby's chance at a cover story. And, just maybe, a second chance for the former sweethearts' own story!

Get 4 FREE REWARDS!

We'll send you 2 FREE Books <u>plus</u> 2 FREE Mystery Gifts.

FREE
Value Over
$20

Both the **Harlequin® Special Edition** and **Harlequin® Heartwarming™** series feature compelling novels filled with stories of love and strength where the bonds of friendship, family and community unite.

YES! Please send me 2 FREE novels from the Harlequin Special Edition or Harlequin Heartwarming series and my 2 FREE gifts (gifts are worth about $10 retail). After receiving them, if I don't wish to receive any more books, I can return the shipping statement marked "cancel." If I don't cancel, I will receive 6 brand-new Harlequin Special Edition books every month and be billed just $5.49 each in the U.S. or $6.24 each in Canada, a savings of at least 12% off the cover price, or 4 brand-new Harlequin Heartwarming Larger-Print books every month and be billed just $6.24 each in the U.S. or $6.74 each in Canada, a savings of at least 19% off the cover price. It's quite a bargain! Shipping and handling is just 50¢ per book in the U.S. and $1.25 per book in Canada.* I understand that accepting the 2 free books and gifts places me under no obligation to buy anything. I can always return a shipment and cancel at any time by calling the number below. The free books and gifts are mine to keep no matter what I decide.

Choose one: ☐ **Harlequin Special Edition**
(235/335 HDN GRJV)
☐ **Harlequin Heartwarming Larger-Print**
(161/361 HDN GRJV)

Name (please print)

Address   Apt. #

City   State/Province   Zip/Postal Code

Email: Please check this box ☐ if you would like to receive newsletters and promotional emails from Harlequin Enterprises ULC and its affiliates. You can unsubscribe anytime.

Mail to the **Harlequin Reader Service:**
IN U.S.A.: P.O. Box 1341, Buffalo, NY 14240-8531
IN CANADA: P.O. Box 603, Fort Erie, Ontario L2A 5X3

Want to try 2 free books from another series? Call 1-800-873-8635 or visit www.ReaderService.com.

*Terms and prices subject to change without notice. Prices do not include sales taxes, which will be charged (if applicable) based on your state or country of residence. Canadian residents will be charged applicable taxes. Offer not valid in Quebec. This offer is limited to one order per household. Books received may not be as shown. Not valid for current subscribers to the Harlequin Special Edition or Harlequin Heartwarming series. All orders subject to approval. Credit or debit balances in a customer's account(s) may be offset by any other outstanding balance owed by or to the customer. Please allow 4 to 6 weeks for delivery. Offer available while quantities last.

Your Privacy—Your information is being collected by Harlequin Enterprises ULC, operating as Harlequin Reader Service. For a complete summary of the information we collect, how we use this information and to whom it is disclosed, please visit our privacy notice located at corporate.harlequin.com/privacy-notice. From time to time we may also exchange your personal information with reputable third parties. If you wish to opt out of this sharing of your personal information, please visit readerservice.com/consumerschoice or call 1-800-873-8635. **Notice to California Residents**—Under California law, you have specific rights to control and access your data. For more information on these rights and how to exercise them, visit corporate.harlequin.com/california-privacy.

HSEHW22R3

HARLEQUIN
PLUS

Try the best multimedia subscription service for romance readers like you!

Read, Watch and Play.

Experience the easiest way to get the romance content you crave.

Start your **FREE TRIAL** at
<u>www.harlequinplus.com/freetrial</u>.